A SPY'S FATEFUL BOND

BOOK ONE
THE FAE KING DUOLOGY

TM GOODKEY

Contents

To my beloved Husband, who encouraged me to take the risk and publish this book.
To my favourite love story.
Ours.

Author Note

Hello, wonderful people. I am taking a chance on this book!

A couple of things to note: this is my first book, so if you find grammar errors that make you want to scratch your eyes out, I am SO sorry! Please email authortmgoodkey@outlook.com, and I will fix it! Telling me will be a quicker fix than reporting it to Amazon. Thank you!

I also want to mention that I am Canadian and write in Canadian English, so if you find some of the spelling off, it is likely because I am spelling it the Canadian way. Eh!

Again, thank you for taking a chance on a new author. I hope you enjoy this book as much as I have enjoyed writing it!

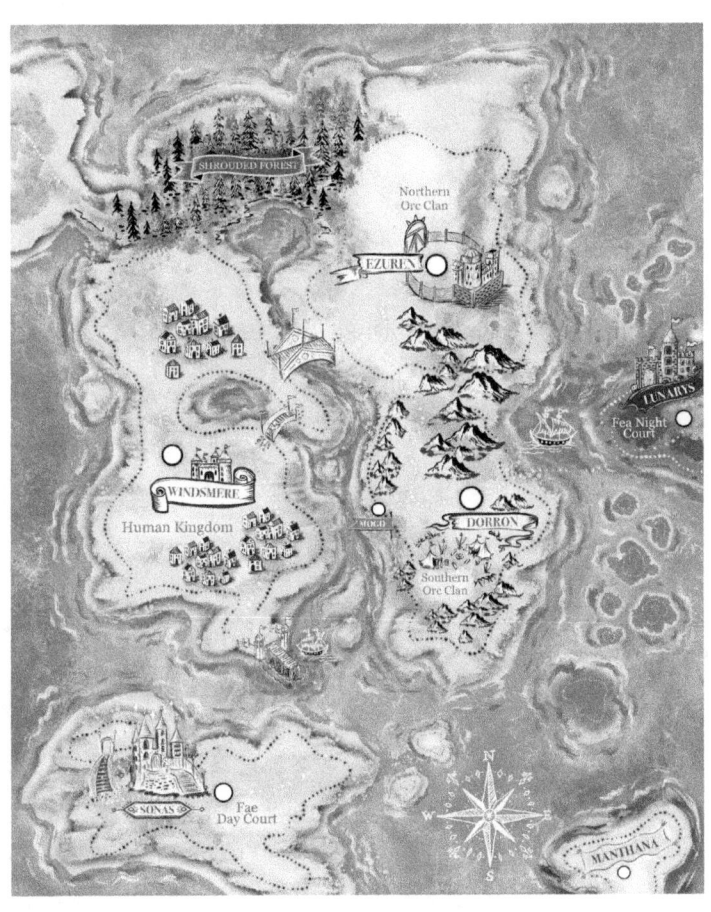

Chapter 1

Emilia

The wind bites against my cheeks, making them raw with every passing breeze. Tugging my cloak tighter, I walk through the village's quiet streets. The days are getting warmer as spring approaches—a welcome relief from the endless snow of winter. Another gust of cold wind pushes past my gathered cloak and into my face, a harsh reminder that winter will not release its hold willingly. That feels fitting, I think to myself, trudging on through the street.

Mud sticks to my boots and stains the bottom of my cloak, eliciting a silent groan as I think of the cleaning that will be required to conceal my efforts tonight. My heart beats faster as I near my intended location. I never wanted to be a spy. I never wanted to come back to the Human Kingdom either, but my mission requires a heartless violation of my wishes.

When my mother abandoned me with my adopted father, I was terrified. He was terrifying in stature, and my six-year-old self didn't know what to do. But my perspective changed over time: he went from terrifying and intimidating to an affectionate protector—a true father. Gratitude fills me as I recall that, if my mother hadn't abandoned me, I wouldn't have the loving father and brother I have now. I probably would have lived in poverty with my mother somewhere in the Human Kingdom, so I am grateful for where I ended up.

Lights flicker above my head, barely illuminating the cobblestone path I'm following. Walking around the village late at night always feels so eerie, but I suppose I shouldn't expect any less from this spy work. I recognise the alleyway on my left, so I quietly turn in and follow the backside of the shops that line the main street. The alleyways are usually quieter and don't have as much light as the main streets—perfect for trying to keep out of sight.

I'm supposed to meet Garrick in the garden just a block away. All the residents use the space to plant vegetables, while the children use it to play. It also happens to be right behind the blacksmith shop in town, where Garrick works. I suppose it's not the worst place to meet for clandestine meetings. One time, we met at a travelling fair—all was going well until someone thought Garrick was the next entertainer in the 'Strong Man' performance. He was not happy about that, but at least no one discovered our true intentions.

Most people are either asleep or at the tavern at this time of night, so there shouldn't be too much foot traffic. Every time I need to meet Garrick, I risk getting caught, and as a result, I'm not sure my heart has beaten a normal rhythm in over a year. If the Duke were ever to find out that one of his daughter's lady's maids was a spy, I would most certainly be tortured and then killed for it—but what am I supposed to do? It was either this or my father would have been killed. Who knows what they're doing to him while they hold him captive even now? I think that's what frightens me the most: not knowing how he is being treated or when I'll see him again. I get snippets of information from Garrick about him, but nothing about how he is really doing or if he is being treated fairly.

I couldn't let them kill him. Even though he may not have contributed to my existence, he is every bit my true father. He was the one who held me when my teenage crush rejected me, the one to wipe away the tears after the local girls teased me. Being a father is more than just blood—it's about being present for your children through every season, good or bad.

But now I recall again the two options they offered before they took him away: become a lady's maid and report what was happening in the Hemmet house, or watch my father die at my refusal. The choice was clear. I packed my bags and, over a year ago, became the intolerable Lady Dahlia's lady's maid.

I round the corner, and a small garden comes into view. There is no lamp lighting this area, only the lights from the windows above illuminating the space. There is a tree in the centre of the space with a swing attached to it, worn and loved by the children in this section of town. Small plots are barren of life in winter's hold, but spring will see them overflow with green leaves and vegetables.

As I approach, I notice a large, imposing figure standing in the shadows. I try to keep my footsteps quiet as I fade into the darkness. As a human, I really shouldn't have extensive training in this kind of deception, but I didn't have a very conventional upbringing. My father and brother taught me how to defend myself and disappear in most situations. That was their preferred reaction in a time of conflict, and I could not agree more. I'm not incredibly strong, and though I am above-average height for a human woman, I still don't stand a chance against someone who knows what they're doing. Self-defence is a last resort, while sneaking away is always my preferred choice. Father always says, 'It's better to keep your head than lose it in a senseless fight.' Easy for him to say—he used to be a warrior and is known for being both strong and brutal during a fight. Nevertheless, I especially appreciate the lessons now.

Garrick steps out from the shadows as he sees me approach. He is a sturdy man, over a head taller than me, and built like a brick wall. His medium-length dark brown hair is haphazardly tied up, with several strands falling around his face. He's covered in soot from working in the blacksmith shop all day, though it doesn't detract from his strikingly pale blue eyes. People often remark that the only way they can tell we are related is by our pale blue eyes.

"Emilia, are you okay? Why was it so urgent to meet?"

"The Duke is preparing for some guests from the capital. The servants are talking about them arriving shortly after we leave for the Day Court. Apparently, they are coming to discuss the upcoming war—the entire house is on edge."

"Do you think they are going to discuss betraying Gormash?"

"I don't know, but it seems possible. All I could find out was that the men coming are some of the King's top advisors. One is currently in the Northern Clans and will return from there to give a report."

"Dak." He curses. "Did you get any names?"

"No. The attendant to the Duke overheard him talking about how these guests would progress the plans to invade the Southern Clans. He also overheard him saying that the King wants an extra regiment called in to invade the Northern Clans simultaneously. I'm unsure if they really know how fortified the Northern Clan is, and unfortunately, I won't be around when they visit."

Garrick takes a deep breath as he digests the information. "Good work, Emilia. I'll send out a hawk to inform our contact. When do you leave for the Day Court?"

"In two weeks."

"Alright. I have arranged to arrive at the blacksmith shop in the lower city of Sonas before you arrive. Come to the blacksmith the day you arrive. We will decide where to meet after that."

"Of course I will." My hands fidget, revealing how worried I am, but Garrick grabs my arm to stop me from turning away. I look at my brother, a sense of sadness filling my heart: sad for our situation and sad that our life has ended up like this.

"Be careful. The Day Court has its own issues right now. Apparently, there have been some unexplained murders in Sonas, creating a troublesome situation. We must remember that our responsibility is to collect as much information about what the humans are up to, but that's it. Hopefully, it will soon be enough and we can go home."

I squeeze his hand and shut my eyes, taking a shaky breath. Tears spring to my closed lids, and I try desperately to control my emotions. Even my lips threaten to betray me as they wobble with emotion.

"Garrick, I just want to go home. I want to see Father." He pulls me into a hug, and my head hits the middle of his chest. I wrap my arms around his waist, which is so large that my arms barely reach fully around his back. I hold tight and soak up his comfort. One day, I won't have to serve the Hemmet house. One day, I can wake up in my little room in our little house on the outskirts of our village, where the mountains sit high in the sky, and the sounds of the river pass by my bedroom window. One day, my father will be safe. I dream of the day I can be wrapped up in his comforting arms, protected from this maddening land. But then I remember that's exactly what he has already done for me the past nineteen years, and it's my turn now to try to provide that same security. Just a little bit longer. Father will be safe, Garrick will be safe, and we can be a family again.

"I know, Emmy. We'll be home soon." He kisses the top of my head as I step away from him.

"I love you, brother."

"I love you too, Em." I will the burning in my eyes to stop as I turn away from Garrick and head back to the estate. A single tear falls from my eye, and I quickly wipe it away. Exhaustion has seeped into my bones, and all I want to do is go home—my true home. But until I know my father is safe, there is nothing else to do but return and play my part.

After leaving the village, the walk along the road back to the estate is peaceful. The worn, muddy roads are just wide enough for a horse and carriage if you are lucky enough to have one. The fields that line the road sit empty in the winter chill but will be filled with the breathtaking sight of golden, swaying stalks at the height of fall.

Lady Dahlia, my mistress, is headed to the Day Court for the five-day spring celebration, scheduled to end with the spring ball. It's rumoured to be the most beautiful event in all the kingdoms, even better than the High King's ball—though I suspect he would kill someone for even thinking such a thing. This is the first time in over a hundred years that the Day Court has invited the Human Kingdom to such an event. No one knows what changed, just that the Fae King wants to 'improve relations' with the Human King. With all that power at play, many speculate that something bigger is going on.

The Day Court Fae live on the islands off the continent and don't often mix with those of us who live on the mainland. For as long as anyone can remember, they have always had an elitist mindset. The Orc Clans take up the Eastern lands by the mountains while the humans take up the western lands. The Human Kingdom and the Southern Orc Clan border the waters across from the Day Court, and even though it's an uneventful four-hour boat ride, the Fae don't like to mingle with us. Not that I blame them—if my being coerced to be a spy isn't a perfect example of how awful living on the mainland can be, I don't know what is.

The Northern and Southern Orc Clans are constantly at odds. They raid each other's villages, burning fields of food, all in the name of more land and authority. It's a mess. The Human Kingdom is no better. It's a cesspit for crime and corruption. The Human King is always looking for more ways to gain power, maintain said power, and acquire land. Then there is the Night Court. Since their exile to the Shrouded Forest over five hundred years ago, they keep to themselves more than the Day Court does.

Suffice it to say, meriting an invitation to the Day Court capital is a momentous event. Lady Dahlia is constantly talking about catching the King's eye. A few noble women hope they can marry the very single Fae King, but I'm not so sure. The Fae have a severe superiority complex—it's one thing to invite the human nobles to their city for the spring festival, but it's an entirely different thing to marry one. Besides, there hasn't been a mixed marriage in centuries. All the gossip doesn't matter to me, though, because all I want is to return to my quiet village to be with my brother and father. The political matters of this place are not my concern. The safety of my family is all I care about, so if I have to go to the Day Court, so be it. We're one step closer to getting our lives back.

The half-hour walk from the village to the estate where the Hemmets live is quiet, which I am grateful for. Being alone is the only time I feel some semblance of peace. Over the past year, I have become increasingly anxious, startling easily and checking every corner, paranoid that someone is going to catch on. It's simply not good for any facet of my health.

The estate comes into view, illuminated by the moon's cold light and a few scant lanterns lighting the windows. The servant's entrance is beside the stables, so I make my way over there as quietly as possible. The horses snort and whinny as I pass by the stables. The Hemmet House has twenty horses, though most are here for the prestige of having them and not actually to ride. The door to the stables opens suddenly, and my heart pounds out of my chest. Ethan, the coach driver, steps out into the night. He turns and notices me walking up to the castle, and I can already guess at the questions now forming on his lips. I hate this part of being a spy: lying to good people. Ethan is a good person. I wasn't built to deceive and sneak around. For most of my childhood, Garrick teased me about how terrible a liar I was, but that's all changed now. I pick mindlessly at the loose threads on my cloak, a nervous habit that distracts my mind from the conversation ahead.

"Emilia? What are you doing out so late?"

"Oh! Ethan, you scared me! I was just out for a walk. I couldn't sleep and thought the fresh air might do me some good."

He takes in my muddy boots and cloak, assessing whether or not I am telling the truth.

"You shouldn't walk around by yourself. It's not safe." He comes up closer to me and folds his hands in front of himself. I've heard through the servant gossip that he is interested in me, but the sentiment isn't mutual. He is a wonderful man, kind, and an animal lover to boot, but I have more important things to worry about right now. I'm not adding falling in love to the list of things I need to do.

"I know, I'm sorry. I'll walk the halls next time."

"If you ever want to go for a walk outside, I don't mind accompanying you." His soft hazel eyes look at me, and I get the feeling he is trying to offer more to me than a walking companion. I inwardly grimace, but I smile a little despite myself.

"Thank you, Ethan. I'll keep that in mind for another time, but I think I'll return to my room. The fresh air accomplished what I hoped it would."

"Of course. I'm heading in myself. May I escort you?"

"Thank you, that's very kind of you." I don't want to be rude. Ethan walks me to the lady's maid quarters, where we awkwardly say goodnight.

Lying in my small bed, I mull over what's to come. If what I heard was true, then maybe after this war, they will release my father and let me go back to our village. Perhaps that's just wishful thinking. Sigrid snores away in the bed next to me. The morning will be here soon, and I know I need all the rest I can get before tending to Lady Dahlia's incessant needs. As I drift off, my mind ponders what the Day Court will look like. I heard

Sonas, the capital city, is filled with impressive buildings that shine in the sun. At least there is that to look forward to.

Chapter 2

Timas

One Year Prior

The crowd parts as I walk into the small house in the lower city. It's uncommon for the King to show up at a lower-class Fae home, but I need to see this myself.

"Your Majesty, the deceased's name is Balo Castor. He was bonded to Nilina. They have one child."

The modest house is decorated with knick-knacks and trinkets, with flowers lining the windows and ceilings. It's small but feels like a home that has been lived in and loved. The Fae man lies on the ground, eyes closed with a slit across his neck. He wouldn't have even been able to scream with how deep the cut is. Nothing is out of place. Nothing overturned to show signs of a struggle. Whoever did this is a professional, just like all the other times. The poor man was surprised by the attack.

"Does his bonded have any idea why he would be attacked?" The guard, ever professional, folds his hands in front of him.

"No, Your Majesty. She says that he is a well-respected member of the community. He works for a farmer just outside of

Sonas, tilling the fields and harvesting in the fall. He works long hours but always comes home happy to be with his family. The neighbours also say he is kind and compassionate, willing to help anyone who asks."

My stomach turns, making me feel nauseous. Innocent Fae people are being slaughtered for no apparent reason. This has been going on for far too long. The first murder happened a couple of months ago. Everything was normal until a report came in that there was a murder in the lower city. At first, it was thought to have been an isolated incident. It was still strange, though, that the victim never fought back. Each death since has been similar. Stealth kills, never in the same place and not specific to class—some are in the lower class, some in the middle, and some in the upper. No one is safe. It doesn't make sense. What is the point of all this? The goal? The purpose? It wasn't until a week ago that we had a breakthrough, but it came at the cost of my father's life when he was assassinated in his room. The difference is the note that was left on the bedside table:

'Your time is coming; you will pay for the sins you have committed against us. Your time of ruling is coming to an end.'

The emblem at the bottom of the note helps give us context: a crescent moon surrounded by seven stars—the symbol of the Night Court.

At one point, the Fae people were ruled and governed by the joint monarchs of the Day and Night Court. Over five hundred years ago, the Night Court monarchs and their people were exiled to the Shrouded Forest on the continent for the civil war they started. No one has heard from them in five hundred years, but now it seems they've chosen to break their silence with this note left by my father's dead body.

"Help the family with the burial and rites. Give them money to cover the expenses. If they need assistance, I will take care of it."

"Yes, Your Majesty." The guard bows and turns to talk to someone else. Walking back into the street, my guards push the crowd back to give me room. I climb up into the carriage and head back to the palace. The sun beats down on my face, warming me, but it doesn't touch the cold I still feel inside. My magic crackles under my skin as I think about my citizens and the terror they must be feeling right now.

"Timas... if you're not careful, you will blow this carriage up." Milori, my second in command and only friend, sits across from me in the carriage. I flex my hands and try to take deep breaths.

"This is getting out of hand. There is no warning for these attacks and no commonality between the victims. It's random and senseless. They are trying to destabilise the Court... and doing an excellent job of it."

We pass by children playing in the street, laughing and happy. But behind them are their parents, whispering and staring at the royal carriage. The people's confidence in the royal family and in me is deteriorating. It's destabilising the peace we've had for hundreds of years.

"We know who's doing it. We just need to figure out how to stop it," Milori says while attentively watching everything and everyone. "The advisors are waiting for you."

I close my eyes because my advisors have been no help whatsoever in this situation.

"Fine. I will meet them when I return." I'm already anticipating the control it will require to remain calm in their presence.

***

The only sound I can hear is my shoes hitting the floor as I walk towards the meeting chambers. It's the same place where the King has been meeting with his advisors for thousands of years, though I've only been King for a decade. Living up to my father's example has been challenging, but my people deserve a good monarch who cares about them and their needs. Father was stepping back to spend the rest of his years together with Mother without the burden of the crown. My mother has always wanted a quieter life, so my father stepped back and let me rise to the throne. They thought they had many more years together, but that was not in their fates.

At the time, this also means he can be an advisor. The Day Court values the thoughts and opinions of the advisors. Father said that, without them, we would fall into the ways of the Night Court. The most significant difference between the Day Court and the Night Court is how our monarchy is run. The Night Court believes in an absolute monarchy. The King has the final say on everything, which includes going against the people and his advisors if he wishes.

The Day Court, on the other hand, has always believed in a consultative monarchy. We depend on our advisors and people to make good policies that will both represent and aid the Fae people as a whole. In some circumstances, the advisors can supersede the King, but it has never been needed before, and I don't plan on requiring it during my reign. The Day Court Kings have always heeded their advice and looked out for the people.

The guards open the double doors leading to the meeting chambers. In the centre of the room sits a large round table with the five advisors. Milori stands off in the corner, watching everyone. I walk to the front of the room where the King's chair is—my chair—and sit down. Zilor is the first to speak.

"Your Majesty, what is the news?"

"Another murder in the lower city. A bonded male with a child, nothing left behind, no disruption to the room—a quick kill. The streets are tense." Estola speaks next.

"What does the Night Court want? Nothing has come from them for hundreds of years, and now this! They took our late King to make their statement, but killing the citizens just shows how mad they truly are."

I sit straighter in my chair and address the five. "The people may be random, but these acts have a purpose: destabilising the monarchy and the people's trust in the royal family. They are, unfortunately, doing a decent job of it. We need to consider the words of the seer." A chorus of disapproving noises comes from my advisors. Of course, they don't want to consider what the seer has to say. I don't want to consider what she says either, but she has seen the future, and we can't simply ignore that.

Raza'l has always been the most outspoken about this: "There is no need to include humans in Fae business. They have no value and will only cause trouble for the Fae people."

"We already have troubles, Raza'l. We have yet to catch the murderer or murderers, and they strike with such efficiency that they are in and out quickly. We need to go straight to the source. If the Night Court wants my attention, they have it. We need to go to the Shrouded Forest and flush them out. The last scout we sent into the woods has not returned, so we must assemble a lethal group of fighters and go to them." My anger is rising with every word I speak. I feel like I'm failing my people. I am failing my people.

"Your Majesty, I think it is wise to gather intelligence about where the Night Court has set up in the Shrouded Forest. Storming the forest with an entire army seems unwise, seeing as we have no direction or information on the area." Estola is a wise woman and has always maintained a level head in these meetings. I may have advisors, but I am the one to make the final decision.

"Estola is right. I will send in a few more scouts and perhaps an assassin or two to see what information we can find. If we can't glean any information, I will invite the human nobles to the spring festival. Let's hope we find out what we need to do before then."

I don't give them any time to share their opinion—standing and walking out is for the best. I'm already on edge, and I can't balance the 'help' they will try to give me. Milori walks quietly beside me, which is unusual, so he has something to say.

"Out with it, Milori."

He snorts. "What gives it away that I have anything to say?"

"Your lips not moving means you have something to say." He gives a half smile and looks straight ahead.

"What exactly did the seer say?" Turning down another long corridor, I look to see who is around. Unfortunately, the walls have ears, so I walk to my chambers without answering. At least there, I have privacy with the magical barrier surrounding it. Walking into the grand room, I head for the balcony that overlooks the channel separating us from the rest of the continent.

"The seer said that I would find the support I needed within the Human Kingdom, that without it, I would not survive the upcoming trials. But she would not say what trials, and she would not say what kind of support either. All she alluded to was that I should invite them to the spring festival." Leaning over the balcony railing, I rake my hands through my hair. Milori comes and leans beside me.

"That all seems very vague."

"When have you ever known her to speak with clarity? The woman is living in the stars half the time. I can't believe the first major event the Day Court has faced since my coronation needs help from the humans, and I have to face it without my father's counsel." Emotion catches in my throat, causing a lump to form. It's been a week since his assassination. I thought I had a hundred more years with him, but he's gone.

"I'm sorry, Timas," Milori says. Pulling myself together, I stand and watch the sunset in the sky. Looking out at the horizon helps me to feel calm, especially when life never seems to be that way.

"The Night Court will pay for what they have done. And if I need to invite the humans, I will."

Chapter 3

Emilia

"Ouch," I mutter. The needle pricks my finger, causing a little bit of blood to spill out. Quickly, I grab a cloth to stem the flow. The last thing I need is to get blood on Lady Dahlia's lovely blue dress. We have a couple more days to finish mending her gowns before leaving for the Day Court. The door to the bedroom opens, and Sigrid walks in, holding a pair of white satin shoes.

"I finally got the scuff off the top of these shoes. It's a miracle it came out at all. Lady Dahlia has been especially meticulous since planning this trip." She walks into the room, puts the shoes into a box, and prepares them for our trip. Thankfully, the bleeding has stopped, and I can finish sewing the small hole in her dress.

"She has been exceedingly whiny lately. Did you see her talking to Duke Hemmet last night? She quite literally stomped her foot at him when he said the jewels she wanted wouldn't make it in time because, apparently, the large chest of jewels she currently has is not enough." I still can't believe what I saw last night. How can a grown woman act like a child? She may only be twenty-one, but with the amount of education and classes on etiquette the woman has taken, you would think she would act with some grace. I'm twenty-five, raised in a small village, and even I know that what she was doing was disgraceful.

"I wish I could say that was a one-time event, but she has been like that since she was small." Sigrid shakes her head and grabs a dress out of the closet, preparing it for the trip.

"You know, I've never asked you how long you've worked for the Hemmets. Sometimes it sounds like you have been with them for decades, but that can't be right, can it?" Her smile is sweet and genuine, as it usually is. I know she is over fifty, but I can't imagine her serving this family for that long. I myself have only been here a year and regularly want to pull my hair out.

"I've been here since I was twenty-one. At first, I worked in the kitchen as a runner, fetching water, logs, and such. I eventually worked my way up to the position of lady's maid. I prefer this to the jobs I started with, even though Lady Dahlia can be challenging."

"Wow, that's a long time. What made you decide to work here?"

"I didn't have a choice, really. My husband died that year, and I needed to find a job to survive. I had no family to help support me because I had run away to marry him. Options were limited, and the Hemmet house provided room and board. It seemed like the best option." I was struck speechless. She was a widow at such a young age.

"Oh, Sigrid, I am so sorry." She continues to fold the dress so that it won't wrinkle too much on our trip.

"Oh, enough about that. That was over thirty years ago. My life is here now. The staff is my family." My heart breaks for her—she has lost so much. I may be forced to be away from my father, but I still have my family and still see my brother.

Standing, I walk over to her and embrace her. She returns it with as much feeling as I provide.

"Thank you for sharing your story with me. I'm sorry I haven't taken more interest in you. You have been so kind to me since I arrived, showing me what to do and correcting my mistakes. You are a kind and wonderful woman. You have no idea how much I appreciate you." She smiles at me and pats my face.

"That's what I'm here for, dear. Now, we need to get Lady Dahlia's evening dress ready. Lady Monson is supposed to be leaving shortly, and we will need to get her ready for dinner." Nodding, I return to mending the dress, which doesn't take too long.

A short time later, Lady Dahlia barges into the room.

"Lady Monson is so irritating. All she does is talk about herself. She is so self-obsessed. Very undignified." She flops down onto the bed unceremoniously and exhales loudly. I look over at Sigrid, who is subtly shaking her head. It's astonishing how this woman can live in such a delusional state. Lady Dahlia sits up and walks over to the vanity, pushing and pulling her hair.

"Now, I need to look immaculate for tonight's dinner. Daddy has invited Duke Gerard's son for supper. I need him to become obsessed with me to prove to Lady Phylis I can sweep her man off his feet. Of course, I don't want him to be interested in me—that position is strictly reserved for the King of the Day Court. Oh, Daddy will be so proud of me when he hears I will be the next Queen of the Day Court." Admittedly, Lady Dahlia is a gorgeous woman. She has lovely dirty blonde hair with doe eyes and the body type all men seem to like, but the inside of her is ugly. Hopefully, the King is smart enough to truly talk with her and not be distracted by her beauty. Although that's a bit laughable, as the Fae people are not known to take humans as spouses—or their 'bonded', as they call them. The Fae people are very pretentious. They have always preferred their people over any other race. They live on the islands, isolated from the continent that holds the humans, Orcs, and exiled Night Court Fae.

"What are you doing, Sigrid?! I said to grab the green dress! Are you deaf? Unbelievable. If Daddy didn't feel he owed you for staying with us for so long, I would have you thrown out. You're getting too old for this job anyway. Emilia! I want you to use the silver pin for my hair tonight."

If I didn't need this job to keep my father alive, I would say or do something that might get me killed—and at this moment, it is a tempting thought. In the village where I grew up, you didn't disrespect those older than you, whether they worked for you or not. Deep breath, Emilia—you need this job.

After we got Lady Dahlia dressed, we were excused to have our meal. Sigrid didn't say much, but she never does. She is too kind. I've never seen her get mad, as she has more patience than anyone I have ever met. I suppose that's not saying much. People where I come from are quick to anger—a lot quicker than most places.

The kitchen is busy with dinner service in progress, but the food for the staff is sitting on the small table on the far wall. Collecting a plate and some food, I find a seat in the storage room beside the kitchen. Some days, I just need some breathing room, and today is one of those days. This life is very different from how my life used to be. My days were spent in the store portion of my father's blacksmith shop. He was known for his craftsmanship. I was content to work and live with him, though maybe it was a bit unusual that I hadn't found a spouse yet. There have been a few offers of marriage and even one from a young man who was quite sweet, but I could never do it. Something never felt right. It always felt like I was waiting for something. Then everything changed the day my father's kidnappers burst into the house. I may have been dreaming of starting my own family at some point, but at that moment, my family was being threatened, and that became my focus.

The door to the storage room opened, and Ethan walked in, dinner plate in hand.

"I thought I would find you here. Rough day?"

"You could say that, but I'm not entirely sure any day has ever been good working for Lady Dahlia."

Ethan nods and finds a barrel to sit on.

"How was your day?" Do I want to know the answer? No, not really. I feel like it just makes him think he has a chance, but I don't want to be rude. Besides, the best way to get information in a noble house is from the staff. Ensuring I don't lose a relationship is important. I need all the avenues I can get.

"The horses have been thoroughly cleaned, and the carriages have been looked over in preparation for the trip. So, busy." I give a small smile and return to eating.

"Are you excited to go to Sonas?" I shrug because I really could not care less, and I want to go home. I want to see the mountains that surround my village, but those are dreams that I fear will never be realised.

"I suppose. I heard Sonas is beautiful, which will be exciting to see."

"I still can't believe we are going. For hundreds of years, the Fae have told everyone on the continent that we are good for nothing, beneath them and their special powers. Something is going on with this invitation, I just don't know what. Besides, I've heard they still haven't solved the murders in their city. They've been trying for a year to get control of it with no success. For a race of people who have powers, you would think they could figure out who is murdering their citizens and stop them." I nod along because I don't have an opinion one way or another. What happens in their city is their issue. My priorities don't lie there.

"Don't worry, though. I'll be there for the time Lady Dahlia is, so I'll look out for you." His smile is sweet. He is a good-looking man, but he has never made anything resembling butterflies fly in my stomach. He's just... nice. Ugh, what's wrong with me? You live under constant stress. That's what's wrong with you. I finish my meal and take my dishes into the kitchen. Lady Dahlia will return to her room to freshen up before heading to the lounge after their meal. It's better if I'm there to deal with her behaviour than Sigrid—she's already spent enough time dealing with that woman.

Chapter 4

Timas

"King Timas, please come in." I walk into the royal seer's chambers, taking in the dark curtains and furniture that decorate the sitting room as incense fills the air. I think the seer mentioned once it was called Aloeswood, which is good for meditation—a fact I don't need to know. Large paintings of seers long since dead hang on the walls, and I have always found their cloudy, white eyes disturbing. This particular seer has been around for almost five hundred years, serving me and my father before me. The last time I sat with her, she told me I needed to 'seek the humans' to solve my problem. 'Absolutely insane,' or at least that's what I thought. But now the body count has increased to fifteen of my best spies and three of my best assassins, not counting all the people who have returned from the trip and have lost their minds.

"Would you care for tea or prefer to get right to it? I see you have returned to perhaps heed my advice?"

My shoulders tense. Does she think I am some petulant child who is not listening to her? A King must do his due diligence. I am not just hoping it will resolve itself—I have been working hard trying to solve this problem. Involving ourselves with the humans has never ended well, not to mention the council has been pushing back harshly on the idea that humans need to be involved at all. The trade agreements are enough for them.

It is well-known that we, the Fae, believe we are better than the humans and the Orcs. I confess this to be an accurate sentiment, but I try not to convey any conceit about it. I must show some sense of acceptance, seeing as I am the face of the Day Court. The Fae people are more refined and intelligent than the races of the continent—even the Night Court, before their exile, could claim that. For hundreds of years, we have sought ways to deal with our problems that don't include gathering an army and conquering, though that might be the way of the past now.

The murders have not stopped, though they aren't as frequent as they first were. We instituted stricter protocols for entering Sonas, requiring rigorous inspections before entering the city by the port. But it continues, and I am at the end of my patience even with the council. My people are not safe or at peace, and if I have to raise an army, I will do so in order to protect them.

I have tried every other way we could think of—inviting the humans might be our best chance at this point.

"Sit, sit." I breathe out my annoyance and go and sit on one of the high-back plush chairs.

"I knew you would return. You were not ready to hear what I had to say last time." The seer fiddles with her dress as she gets comfortable.

"Then why did you say anything at all?"

"You needed to feel like you did all you could before returning to me," she says with a cheer that I do not feel. She is such an odd woman dealing with the future. You would think she would be cold and off-putting, but she has always been very cheery, but in an eerie way.

"Seer, I do not wish to play games. How do I stop them from killing my people? Stop them from trying to kill me?"

"Yes, they do seem rather determined to kill you. It's interesting, don't you think? You are the most powerful Fae King we have seen in centuries. As to your question: the first step, as I had said, is to connect with the humans. You need their support."

"I do not know how that is going to root out the Night Court and stop this senseless slaughter. They won't even tell us what they want. They just kill indiscriminately. In addition, you haven't explained what kind of support I need from the humans. Your vague words lead me to no answers—more guessing than resolution."

"Yes, it is rather pointless without a reason, though maybe their reason is more than you know." What? Did that even make sense? "As you know, looking into the future is difficult. There are many possible outcomes, and I can't tell you exactly what will happen."

I feel my frustration rising with every word she speaks, causing a mild headache. I'm trying to take deep breaths, but my power is building up, and if I'm not careful, I will unintentionally expel it from my body. The floor starts to shake as I try to rein in the raw energy that pulses through me. All I seek is a straight answer, a clear path! It has been over a year of this, and I am getting to the end of myself.

Electricity crackles under my skin. If I looked in a mirror, I know my eyes would be darkened with faint lines of lightning crossing them. I like to think I don't get angry easily, but this has been going on for far too long. The seer has information, and I swear she is being deliberately evasive.

"My King, I do not mean to agitate you—this is just the facts of trying to see the future. To give too much and the fates would be mad, and to give too little, well... actually, giving too little doesn't matter because the future would just be the future. Never mind, here is what I can tell you. You must invite the eligible women of the Human Kingdom to the spring festivals."

"What! Why?"

"This is the first step in getting the support you need. You will find something valuable, and without it, you will be unable to stop the storm coming your way."

I lean my arms on my knees and run my hands through my hair. The last thing I want to do is have several humans wandering the palace at such a critical time for my people. Opening our borders could also allow for more assassins to come in unnoticed. The 'sun' forbid one of them is attacked here, and I have to explain that to the High King.

Plus, the spring festival is a time for the Fae people to celebrate the new life about to grow on the islands and the time when Fae couples often come together and find love. This would be the first time humans have joined us for this festival, at least as long as I have lived. The last time I remember them coming was when my father invited a delegation for a visit over one hundred years ago. I was one hundred and fifty at the time and spending way too much time trying to avoid royal responsibility.

Pushing the memory of that conversation out of my mind, I focus on today. It's been three months since I spoke to the seer, and today is the day that the nobles from the Human Kingdom will be arriving. The sun rises in the east over the channel, reflecting its light and causing it to dance on the waves. The smell of roses and lavender floats through my bedroom window, reminding me that not everything in this world is frustrating. It's peaceful this early in the morning, and I try to soak up what little of it I can before it gets busy. Spring has finally come to the Day Court, and the Spring Festival is about to begin—an exciting time for the people. I've been anxiously awaiting this festival. Hopefully, this will go a long way in allying with the Human Kingdom. It's the only thing I could come up with from the advice the seer gave me. Though I have no idea how it will help, this 'support' is supposed to be somewhere in the Human Kingdom.

Inviting the most influential human figures and eligible women to our festival proved to be an excellent opportunity to make connections and show good faith to the High King. Despite my council's objections, I don't see any other way to put on such a display. We have sequestered ourselves away from the continent—perhaps this will show our desire for an alliance. Maybe we need them as a proxy army? I am unsure. They share a border with the Shrouded Forest—perhaps that is the way we need to get in. It makes more sense to do that than go through the constantly unstable Orc lands on the continent's eastern side.

Despite the opportunities, never in my two hundred and fifty years did I imagine I would invite the humans into our city. They have historically been greedy and power-hungry, and for a race that has no special powers or abilities, they think rather highly of themselves. I am still determining how this will help us, but I'm desperate and out of options.

These murders are causing tension between me and my people. They are losing faith in my abilities to protect them. I can't blame them, but I am determined to be the King they need. Bringing the humans here was a good idea—I can only pray it is not a mistake.

Lost in my thoughts, I hear a knock on the door of my chambers.

"Enter!" The guard stationed in front of my door walks in and hands me a message orb. He bows deeply and exits the room.

Turning the orb around in my hand, it floats above my palm as I start to read its message, pulsing with light on each word.

"Your Majesty, the first of the human caravans have arrived. The council requests a meeting with you before you attend to other duties." The orb puffs in the air, leaving a light mist in its wake. It is a faerie device used to send messages and can only be heard by the person it is intended for. It is a very secure device for private messages, though I wonder why my chamberlain wouldn't tell me directly. Perhaps it is because we have so many new guests arriving.

The door opens again, and my second-in-command, Milori, walks in.

"Good morning, Your Majesty." Glaring at him, I head towards my closet to grab my clothes. "Oh, stop being such a grumpy kitten. We have guests. This should be fun!"

"First, kittens aren't grumpy, they're cute. Second, this is not fun. This is stressful. You should be far more stressed than I am, seeing as you oversee the security of the ENTIRE palace."

"Did you just say cute? You are a softy at heart." He clasps his hands and bats his eyes at me. What an idiot.

"Don't make me regret the choice to make you my second in command."

"Who else were you going to choose? No one else would put up with your insanity day in and day out."

"I'm the King. It would be required whether they like to put up with me or not."

"Obviously. Well, I came by to see if you need to spar—perhaps releasing some of that pent-up stress would be healthy."

"As much as I want to best you yet again in a sparring match, the council has requested a meeting." Milori groans at that. Honestly, his behaviour is unprofessional, but he only acts this way around me and never in front of others.

"What do they want? We know they aren't happy and that we don't trust them. Let's simply ignore them and do what we want."

"As enticing as that sounds, I refuse to act like the Night Court. The Night Court King did not value outside input, and they were exiled for it."

"That is a very short and holey summary of what happened at the Night Exodus."

Grabbing my robe, I slip my arms through the holes. "That may be, but I refuse to go down that slippery slope. So I will hear what they have to say, and then I will spar with you, though I don't know why you like losing so much."

"Ha, just you wait! I have a few new tricks up my sleeve."

"You know, I think you need to find a bond. You spend way too much time getting beaten by your King."

"I'll get bonded when you do—which is when, by the way? Rumour has it you are picking a human bond! How scandalous." He whispers that last bit.

"You know I am waiting for my Spirit bond." Milori goes quiet at that. There hasn't been much I have ever really wanted. I have dedicated my life to my people, but one thing I have always wanted is my Spirit Bond. The elusive bond that connects two Faes so wholly together that nothing can pull them apart. When their spirits intertwine, this unbreakable bond between the two is formed. It has been an increasingly rare occurrence among our people since exiling the Night Court. Scholars have guessed it is because our spirit bonds are in the Night Court, but those are only theories. I do not want a chosen bond—I want the unbreakable love of my spirit bond.

"You'll find her, Timas." I nod because, after two hundred and fifty years, I'm beginning to lose hope. But that's not what I need to focus on right now. Right now, I need to focus on the human caravans and the council.

"Let's go. Let's see what they have to say," I say to Milori as I head to the door. This is going to be a long week.

Chapter 5

Emilia

The journey to the Day Court was long and arduous. I'm relatively certain the lower part of my body will be permanently numb from this journey. It turns out that getting to ride on a ship wasn't all that exciting because I spent most of it surrendering my breakfast into the sea—four hours of my head spinning and the sailors chuckling at my discomfort. In my defence, I have never been on a ship before. How was I to know that I needed to look at the horizon to prevent the sickness? Ugh, I still feel a little bit disgusted. Sigrid was kind enough to give me a few pieces of mint leaves to chew on, which seems to be helping. Thank the heavens.

After docking, dock workers and palace staff arranged our things and put us into the most beautiful carriage. The carriage was in the shape of a dome made from crystal, and as the sun hit its surface, beautiful colours danced around within it. Large, stunning white horses pull the carriage, larger than what we have on the continent and far cleaner. The inside of the carriage had plush seating covered in a velvety light blue colour. It all felt so surreal. When the city came into view, my breath was lost yet again. The road was paved with the most beautiful stones that, according to the footman I overheard, even glow at night. The sun charges them, and then they emit a subtle glow, lighting the city in the evening. Flowers and plants of all kinds cover the unpaved grounds. It feels like an entirely different world.

But even with such beauty, there is always ugliness, and you can easily tell that the Fae people didn't want us here. But to no one's astonishment, Lady Dahlia is happily off in a land of delusion, so she doesn't even notice the stares and comments. Oh, to live such a carefree life. Finally, we make it into the castle courtyard, where many human nobles are unloading and heading into the castle.

"Can you believe they invited Lady Sibil to come to this?! And look at what she's wearing! She looks like a poor beggar in those clothes!" Lady Dahlia exclaims to her closest confidant, Lady Jules.

"I bet she is only here to try to entice the King. She is a shameless flirt."

The hypocrisy is apparently lost on these women, as they are both nearly falling out of their dresses. I have a hard time relating to them, though I suppose my job isn't to relate to them but to eavesdrop on them. Pulling up to the main entrance is a sight to behold. The castle itself is enormous, with large glass windows decorating its entirety. With the sun hitting it from behind, you can see the stained-glass patterns in each window. I am sure the hallways are a kaleidoscope of colours, making you feel like you are in a different world. A smartly dressed Fae man comes down to welcome the nobles.

Meanwhile, the help is sorting out their things. Sigrid and I have been informed that we will be on the castle's east side, and they will arrange for the luggage to be delivered there. I quickly walk over to Ethan to inform him of the plan.

"Apparently, they will deliver the luggage to the room. The gentleman over there will be taking it," I say to Ethan, pointing over to the tall Fae man. Ethan gently puts down a large brown trunk and straightens to look at me.

"I see. I guess I will speak with him."

We manage to make it to Lady Dahlia's room and start organising her things, but before long, her entitled self starts whining.

"Well, I suppose this room will have to do." Lady Dahlia has been here for all of ten minutes and is already assessing the quality of the room. This room is one of the most beautiful rooms I have ever seen. The four-poster bed sits against the wall with sheer curtains draping from the sides. The little sitting area with soft pink fabric creates a comfortable space to rest, and the curtains framing the large arched windows look like they are made of the finest material you could buy or make. Her estate isn't nearly as lovely as this place. Some days, I wish she would spend a day in my old village. She wouldn't last a day, and I revel in the thought. Lady Dahlia is ordering the Fae attendants around like they are beneath her, though I suppose she does that to all her staff. I don't know why I thought she would be different with the Fae people. Spoiled doesn't even begin to describe this girl.

"Emilia, this place is lacking. I heard there was a beautiful garden in the castle that rivals the High King's, though I doubt it could compare. I want you to find it and bring me fresh-cut flowers, one of every kind. Also, I have an order ready for pickup in town at the dress shop. Fetch it."

I turn just slightly to see the vase full of beautiful fresh-cut white flowers sitting beside her bed, and because I can't stop talking sometimes, I point that out.

"Lady Dahlia, it looks like the rooms have fresh-cut flowers. Is there something you don't like about it?"

"Emilia, you talk back more than a servant should," she says with her hands on her hips. "Your only job is to do exactly as you are told. White is so boring. I need life; I need colour!" This woman is supposed to be a sophisticated young lady. "When I become queen—because I will—I will have to redecorate these rooms. Daddy will be so proud once he finds out I have caught the eye of the King. With me as the Fae Queen, I'm sure Daddy will be elevated higher in the High King's court. I just need to use all my charms to catch the Fae King."

This woman is delusional. Charm? What charm? I hope I'm there when she finally sees she isn't as impressive as she thinks. She may be a beautiful young woman, but even the money she uses to cover her hideous centre will reveal itself eventually. Besides, we aren't in the Human Kingdom anymore. We are in the Day Court. She may get what she wants when she wants it back at her home, but I have a feeling she won't get the attention she wants here... which will make my job harder. I have no power. I am, as she says, a mere servant.

"Yes, my lady. I will go search for your flowers."

"Good. Sigrid, get a bath drawn; the travel was terrible. I need to be bathed and ready for dinner tonight. Oh, and pull out the red dress, the one that makes my chest look big. That ought to get his attention, and don't forget to grab..."

I roll my eyes and exit the suite as Lady Dahlia continues to yammer on. According to her, this place barely meets her standards. Meanwhile, I grew up in a two-bedroom house in a small village where the smell of wood burning was the fragrance of choice versus the scent of lilacs and roses, which seemed to float in the air in this palace. But as lovely as this place is, I would give anything to be in my old house making venison stew for my family because what a place looks like doesn't make a home—the people inside it do.

The halls are vast, with one side covered in stained glass windows that look down onto the courtyard below. Every twenty feet, a Fae soldier wearing a dark blue uniform and a black sash around the waist stands vigil. Some of them have a sword on their waist; others don't have any at all. I wonder why? All their weapons look like the Orcs have made them. They are strong and lethal. Most Fae, to my knowledge, have some power: fire, earth, wind, metals, and even mind manipulation, but I don't know how to tell who can do what. I also heard something about certain groups having more power than others. I really don't know. Maybe I can ask the servants here to satiate my curiosity. The Orc-made weapons are deadly on their own. Add in the Fae's ability to use magic, and I would not want to meet them on the battlefield. Maybe it's good they have kept to themselves all these years.

I presume the weapons are the finest the Orc Clans make. The Orc Clans live on and around the mountains on the continent, and the metals found in those mountains are strong. Over the years, the Orcs have perfected how to make excellent weapons, and for that reason, they are the major sellers and importers of such things. I heard some Fae have tried to make their own weaponry, but everyone still prefers the ones made by the Orcs.

I have my hands clasped in front of me as I pass each soldier. I have no idea where I am going, but I will take advantage of the opportunity to look around. The castle is massive! We are in the east tower, where all the human guests are staying. Before we made it to Lady Dahlia's room, some of the servants told us the east tower was warded, so we couldn't go anywhere the King did not permit. I can't blame them for taking precautions. It's not like they invited good, hardworking humans to the festival—they invited the rich and powerful, who, more often than not, are corrupt, selfish, and simply terrible human beings all around.

I decide it is best to get Lady Dahlia's order and, while I'm out, go to the blacksmith to find out where to meet my brother. Leaving the castle wasn't all that hard; navigating the city, on the other hand, is a bit confusing. The city seems to shine and sparkle like a crystal chandelier swaying in the sun. The buildings are made of soft grey stone with beautifully carved columns. The upper city is obviously where those with money live. The streets are clean, and the windows are made of clear blue glass, making it look fake with how perfect it is. The lower you go, however, things start to get a bit more crowded. People are dressed in more simple clothing, though much nicer than the simple people in the human or Orc populations. The main square where the shops sit is busy with people wearing elegant and simple clothing. It seems that they have no problem mixing together for shopping. Some shops are intricately designed to show off beautiful jewellery, while another shop is filled to the brim with books. It is an amazing place, and I wish I could explore it. A massive fountain sits in the middle of the square, with two smaller ones on either side. Carts with different coloured fabrics draped over them cover the square. Some sell food, and others sell scarves or wine. They are even selling small flying creatures—maybe they are used as pets? Not all Fae seem to have wings. I heard that only the royal family has them, but perhaps that is wrong.

It doesn't take me long to find 'Sharif's Clothing' and pick up Lady Dahlia's order. Garrick said the blacksmith was in the lower city. Most places put the blacksmith a bit away from the main square so the created dirt and noise don't disturb the shoppers' experience. A lovely Fae woman with pink hair points me in the direction I am supposed to go. Just behind the market square, I see a small shop with a forge and anvil just outside. The wall on the front of the shop holds tools and weapons for sale. Just as I approach, a tall, hulking Orc steps out from inside. He sees me coming and eyes me with suspicion. It isn't within their nature to be trusting, but my brother said to come here, so this must be where he is working.

"Good afternoon, Sir. Is Dorgan Garrick here?" His eyebrows raise just slightly, and if you weren't paying attention, you wouldn't notice, though his shock is evident to me. He must not be expecting anyone, which is odd because Garrick told me to come here.

"Who's asking?"

See, not trusting, but they are loyal. If Garrick said he was supposed to be working here, he would know why I'm here... I hope.

"Someone looking for the hawk," I say.

I speak the phrase Garrick came up with to tell anyone that I was with him. It's an ode to our pet hawk that we now use to send messages back and forth. This time, his brows reach nearly his long braided hairline. His mouth falls open slightly, making his tusks more pronounced. I guess he wasn't expecting someone like me. I would have anticipated Garrick to explain, but apparently not this time. Sometimes, I think he does it on purpose, having the human maidservant coming up to the Orc blacksmith. He thinks he is so funny, but I guess it's better to keep a sense of humour in this crazy time.

"Well, gotta admit I never saw that coming. He isn't here today but wanted me to give you this."

He leans down and pulls out a piece of paper and something wrapped in cloth. He hands me the items and turns back to do his work. There really isn't much to say, so I turn and head back towards the palace. Before I get too far, I find a little spot between buildings to read my note.

Meet me tomorrow before dawn by the docks. There is a small warehouse at the end of the docks, warehouse number twelve. Be safe. PS Father sent you a gift.

I fold the paper, tuck it into my dress, and unwrap the cloth to find a beautifully crafted dagger. The handle is made out of a strong wood with an intricate pattern along the handle. The blade is made of white iron, the strongest metal from the winter mountains and lethal to the Fae. He must be worried about me being in the Day Court because this dagger is made to kill Fae, not just animals, which is what my other dagger is used for. I slip the dagger back into its holder and tuck it under my dress. I will have to make something to attach it to my leg like the other dagger I carry.

After completing all my errands, I head back to the palace to find some of the flowers I am supposed to collect.

Returning and dropping off the clothes for Lady Dahlia didn't take long. She was having tea with another lady from the High King's court, so I'm not harassed further. There are two hours before the dinner, so I should, in theory, have enough time to get those silly flowers and return them so I can help Sigrid.

I make my way into the central portion of the castle, looking for any sign of a garden nearby. Wandering around the halls, looking out the large windows, I hoped to glimpse an outdoor garden space, but I couldn't see one. After walking the same hallway twice, I realised I might need to ask for help. Ugh, this is embarrassing. It's bad enough I've walked past the same guards twice, but now I need to explain that I'm lost. I think they probably already know that.

Just as I'm turning the corner, a very tall man dressed in what looks to be a soldier's uniform is walking towards me. He seems different from all the rest, as he has more intricate designs on his uniform and a single sword swinging from his hip. He has short blonde hair that seems slightly unkempt, giving him a carefree look in stark contrast to his official clothing. His eyes are a beautiful sea-green colour, and his walk alone reveals his importance, aided by how the stationed soldiers bend slightly as he passes. I need to ask for help, but this soldier seems a bit too important. I should look for one of the servants—I'm sure they have the same culture as in the Human Kingdom. Help your fellow servants out; it's basic servant etiquette. But now that I think of it, I haven't seen any servants around. Maybe there are servant corridors like they have in the Human Kingdom. I would much rather ask a maid for help than this very tall, very handsome Fae man. While lost in thought, one of the tall vases that lined the walls and had previously gone unnoticed by me comes into view. One would think I would notice a vase nearly as tall as me, but they would be wrong. I jostle it slightly, squeak, and try to regain my balance, desperately trying to save the (likely extremely expensive) piece of art.

Out of nowhere, strong arms simultaneously keep me from falling and steady the vase. My heart pounds hard, the whooshing sound of blood in my ears making me feel a bit lightheaded. That was close. I don't know the punishment for breaking royal art, but I don't want to find out. Trying to take deep breaths, I look up to see who saved me and the rogue vase. I lift my gaze to be met by those same sea-green eyes sparkling in the sun. Are all Fae men this handsome? The man has his arms wrapped around me, holding me against his chest, and my heart is beating fast for an entirely different reason now. Get it together, Emilia. I have never been in the arms of a man before, excluding hugs from my brother and Father, so this is not a position I find overly comfortable. I push myself away from him to gain some much-needed distance. I turn to look up at him again and profusely apologise to this very important man.

"I... I am so sorry. I wasn't paying attention. I didn't see the vase until it was too late. Please forgive me."

He doesn't say anything at first, which makes me nervous. I don't know what he is thinking, and to quickly try to escape, I tip my head down to show some respect. I hope this is respectful because I really don't know what to do in this situation. Long fingers lift my face to look up, and I stare again into those lovely eyes.

"It's alright. The vase is fine, and I am glad to see you were not injured."

"Yes, I'm sorry. I didn't mean to bother you. You seem like a very important man. Please don't let me hold you up. I... I won't run into any more vases, I promise."

He laughs and lets his hand fall to his side.

"What are you doing here, anyway? I assume you came with one of the caravans from the Human Kingdom?"

"Oh yes, um, I am one of Lady Dahlia's lady's maids. She has requested I get her some fresh-cut flowers from some garden. I am not sure exactly where this garden is, or even if I am allowed to go to it, but if she doesn't get what she wants, she gets... cranky."

He raises one eyebrow and looks at me. I suddenly feel very self-conscious. I mean, I don't think I am horrible to look at, but the white and pale rose dress and apron make me very much a working woman. My hair is falling out of my bun and likely all over the place at this point in the day.

"Well, if she means the royal gardens, they are off-limits to the guests. I was assured that our rooms were adequately decorated with fresh-cut flowers."

Of course they are! Here I am, wandering around in a Fae palace, apparently trying to steal the ROYAL flowers! My face is starting to burn red from utter embarrassment.

"I am so sorry. I had no idea. I really didn't know who to ask, and I haven't seen any servants to ask where I should go. Please forgive me."

I tip my head down and start backing up a bit. This is a disaster. Why couldn't she just be happy with what she was given? Ah, that's right—because she is a pompous, entitled prat. My breathing has become a bit shallow, and I realise I am panicking slightly. What if I get Lady Dahlia in trouble, and then she gets mad at me, and I lose this job and can't save my father?

"Hey, hey, hey. It's okay, just breathe."

I try to take some calming breaths, but as the months have passed, my anxiety has only gotten worse. I was not meant to be a spy. I was supposed to help my father in his shop and maybe one day get married. I was not supposed to be a spy! Lately, I have only become increasingly paranoid and anxious. The longer I do this, the harder it has become—but I won't let my father down. Not now, not ever.

"I'm sorry. Please, if you don't mind telling me where I could maybe grab some flowers. I won't go to the Royal Gardens. Maybe there are some nice weeds I could grab."

This apparently made this handsome man laugh; I mean, I really wasn't joking. There are nice weeds. I'm sure I could convince Lady Dahlia they are exotic or something.

His laugh seems so carefree, just like his hair. "As wonderful as it would be to see you bring weeds back to your mistress, how about I escort you to the royal gardens? I am sure the nobles in the human kingdom are similar to here—always expecting the world and punishing those serving them."

"Oh, so you know what it's like to deal with irritating and delusional nobles."

"I'm afraid so, though my boss can take a joke. He has, on occasion, thrown me off the balcony."

As he starts to lead me back down the hall, I nearly trip over myself. He can't be serious, can he? Surely that must have been a joke, right?

"As in, literally throw you off the balcony?"

He is still laughing at this, which is mind-boggling because I don't think being thrown off a balcony would be fun. Terrifying seems more accurate.

"I'm afraid so. He has a bit of a temper, and I am a glutton for punishment. But it's always so fun to rile him up."

"How are you not dead if he has thrown you off a balcony?"

"Ah yes, I suppose you might not know since you're human. But some of us can fly—we have wings."

And because I have apparently lost my mind entirely, I start trying to look at his back. He has no wings, and his clothes don't even look like they could accommodate them if he did. Coming back to myself, I see that he is looking at me, and obviously, my face heats in embarrassment. He doesn't help by winking at me and walking confidently to our destination. As I reflect on what I've just done, I'm filled with trepidation. Was it rude to look? Did I just insult him by looking for his wings? Ugh, when will this day end?

Before I knew it, we arrived at a beautiful set of dark wood doors with intricate glass, showing the garden on the other side. He pushed the doors open and walked through. A gust of warm air flowed out of the door and hit me in the face, smelling of all things beautiful. The smile on my face was not forced but deeply genuine. I'm not sure of the last time I genuinely smiled.

"Here we are. We can't spend too long here because I need to return to my duties, but you can grab some flowers for your mistress."

My eyes can't seem to comprehend the beauty I am looking at. I am in awe of the multitude of flowers in all varying colours, and I can't believe such a beautiful place exists. A tall willow tree sits in the middle, and bushes upon bushes of gorgeous flowers cover the space. A stone path seems to weave around the flowers, making you feel like you are walking with the flowers, not cutting through them. I have never seen so much beauty in one place. Even back home, there were some flowers in the woods, but nothing like this. I feel like I have stepped into a new world, and I want to stay here forever.

Chapter 6

Timas

I had come into the gardens to get away from everyone. The constant barrage of questions from the council about the humans only angered me, and the never-ending reports of some of the nobles' requests were beyond irritating. I just need a few minutes alone to compose myself before I eviscerate someone. That only happened once, and it wasn't actually a person. It was a chair, but the person in the chair wasn't very happy about being flung across the room. Some days, I wonder if my being the King is a good idea. I know I am powerful, but sometimes I think about how heavy the crown can be. I admired my father for his dedication to the crown, and I can only hope that I will live up to the example that he showed.

As a child, I often used my power to keep people at a distance. Milori was the only one who wasn't scared of me and would come around and even spend time with me. He thinks I am dramatic. I think he has a death wish. As I got older and took the required royal classes, I was taught the proper behaviour of being a prince and what it would take to be a king. Apparently, I have to be pleasant and talk to everyone.

Sighing, I go and sit on the bench under the willow tree. It's one of my favourite places to retreat. I feel hidden behind the tree's long, swaying branches. Maybe some quiet will help me handle these demanding humans and the council's expectations. Not ten minutes into my peaceful moment, the doors to the garden open, and in walks my friend and captain of the guard, Milori. He is supposed to be arranging patrols for the upcoming dinner, not shirking his duties and coming into the gardens. The irony that this is exactly what I'm doing currently is not lost on me; however, as King, I am allowed this freedom. I hear him speaking to someone else as I stand to talk to him. I didn't initially hear what he said, but as I got closer, I could hear this voice calling to me like a siren calling its prey. It's like a beautiful song pulling me in, a strong current running through me. All I know is that I need to get closer. I need to see the face of the woman with such a magical voice.

"I can't thank you enough for letting me come here. You are the saviour of vases and poor lady's maids. You have been so very kind to me and... I don't even know your name?"

"My name is Milori, and it has been my pleasure to help you. And your name is?"

"Yes, of course! My name is Emilia."

"A beautiful name for a beautiful woman." A growl escapes my throat after hearing him call her beautiful. It's completely irrational, but I can't seem to control the anger that comes over me. All I can think of is that I am supposed to call her beautiful, not Milori. I try to shake off whatever is possessing me and focus back on what they are saying. The way I am acting doesn't make sense, and Milori lifts his head, slowly turning to look directly at me. He is tall enough to see me over the bushes that surround the tree. It also helps that the Fae people have excellent eyesight, so it's not difficult for him to see where I am standing. The small human can't see me, which explains her next question.

"Wha-what was that noise? Is there an animal in here? Because if there is, I will face the wrath of my mistress and not pick any flowers." Milori doubles over, holding his stomach and laughing at her comment, knowing full well that the animal she is referring to is none other than the King of the Day Court.

"My dear Emilia, he can be an animal sometimes, but nothing for you to worry about. You pick your flowers."

"Okay...?" I can hear the hesitation in her voice, like she doesn't believe him, but this mistress of hers must be scarier if she is worried about this 'animal' but still stays to pick some flowers. An intense need comes over me—I need to see her. I move as quietly as I can to the other side to get a glimpse of the woman who has been quickly ruining my senses. I finally see her leaning over and collecting some flowers on the other side of a hibiscus bush.

The sight nearly knocks me off my feet. Can the beauty of a woman make you feel lightheaded? I feel like I am being swallowed up by her stunning allure. Never in my two hundred and fifty years have I ever seen such beauty. She is taller than an average female human but still significantly shorter than me. Her beautiful brown hair falls out of the bun she must have put up this morning. The dress she is wearing is not at all flattering, but somehow, she still looks like she is wearing the finest silk. I immediately decide that I will buy her the finest of fabrics—she won't need to wear those terrible clothes anymore. I can't see the colour of her eyes, which irritates me, but I mostly want to find out what she smells like. This overwhelming feeling of rightness hits me straight in the heart. Is this my spirit bond? Could she really be right in front of me, completely oblivious to my presence? I have an uncontrollable urge to scoop her up and lock her in my room until she agrees to be my bonded.

That urge strikes me like a heavyweight—what is wrong with me? My magic pulses just under my skin like it is trying to leave me and get to her. This has to be my spirit bond... a human spirit bond. What am I going to do?

I must speak to her. Milori notices me standing and staring at the beauty in my garden and folds his arms over his chest. His smirk is exceptionally aggravating and makes me want to do irrational things, like tossing him into the rose bush. Still, I don't want to scare my precious flower, so I raise an eyebrow, indicating he should introduce me.

"Emilia, you know how I told you about my boss?"

"Hmm? Oh, you mean the irrational one who threw you off the balcony? I hope he pays you well, by the way. I'm not sure even I would put up with that, even if I did have wings."

My shock isn't hidden on my face—he did not tell her I did that! Milori barks out a laugh while staring right at me, and I'm convinced he needs another flight lesson off my balcony.

"The very one. Well, it's your lucky day. You get to meet him."

"What?! No, I don't want to be thrown off a balcony! I don't even have wings!"

"I don't think he will throw you off a balcony, but I suspect he will want to... you know what, never mind."

I am going to do more than throw him off a balcony. At this point, he is scaring my precious flower. I walk out from behind the bush, and she whips around to stare at me wide-eyed. Her eyes are this pale blue that I could get lost in forever. The closer I get to her, the stronger her sweet scent becomes. I put on my most charming smile as I bow just slightly. This is my spirit bond. I found her, and I won't ever be letting her go.

"Emilia, this is King Timas of the Day Court. Timas, this is Emilia."

"It is a pleasure to meet you, my flower."

She mouths the word flower, likely thinking I'm a bit crazy for giving her a nickname, but I can't help it. She realises she is staring and bows deeply, nearly dropping her flowers as she speaks.

"Your Highness, or Majesty, um, yes, a pleasure to meet you." She is adorable. I step closer to her because I have to—something compels me to. I'm so close I could reach out and touch her, which I desperately long to do, and in a moment, my whole world comes together. This is the woman I have been waiting for for so long. She is everything to me. A Fae person is lucky to find their spirit bond, and here I am standing in front of her. I've truly found her.

I guess I will have to thank the seer and possibly apologise for my poor attitude. I reach out to help her stand up straight. She still looks frightened, but the pink on her cheeks tells me I might be affecting her just as she is affecting me. I slip my hand along her jaw and look into her gorgeous eyes.

"You are beautiful, my flower."

"I um... well... uh... what?" she stutters out.

"I said you are beautiful and will be my queen."

"I hit my head and am dreaming. This can't be real. I'm just going to close my eyes and open them again, and I will be in that horrible palace serving the dreadful Lady Dahlia. Yes, that's what's happening." The tingles that erupt down my fingers through my arm are like a newfound addiction, an insatiable craving that can only be sated by her. She doesn't believe me, but I will prove to her that this is real. I don't know how the bond will work on a human, but I will show her I am worthy of her time. Her eyes snap open again, and I smile at her antics. She seems to find her words as disbelief crosses her face, and she mumbles out,

"This can't be real."

"It is, darling, very real."

"You are very kind, but um, I should go. My mistress will already be upset with me for taking so long. I—I need to go." She starts backing up and nearly falls over a bush. I rush forward, grabbing her by the waist and pulling her close, feeling her breathing heavily. Our eyes meet, and I swear I hear her suck in her breath.

"You do not need to return to this mistress of yours. I will take care of you now. You don't need to work anymore."

"WHAAA?! No! No, I must!"

She pushes herself out of my arms and runs out of the garden, leaving me standing there in complete shock. Not just from her sudden absence, but no one has ever run from me when I've wanted their attention. I've never experienced someone literally fleeing from me. Never experienced the sting of rejection. Never heard 'no' to any request. So many firsts in such a short period of time. My feet are stuck to the floor, even though I want to run after her.

"Well, nice going, Timas—swept her right off her feet."

Power pulses through me suddenly. I shoot my hand out and send Milori into the rose bushes.

"Ugh, Timas, come on! Why the rose bush? There are so many thorns! Ouch!"

Turning on him, I walk over to his tangled body in the rose bush.

"Just be glad I am so forgiving right now."

"We need to talk about your understanding of forgiving."

"That's my spirit bond, Milori!"

"Yes, I assumed as much from the growl and all-around lovesick look on your face. My congratulations, friend."

"She ran away!"

"I mean, have you looked at yourself? I would, too. You're ugly." He had just exited the bush, so I sent him into the one beside it. He is so very annoying, but he is my only friend, so I can't kill him. The gardener is going to have to work a miracle on those plants, though.

"Where is she going?"

"Ouch! You know, part of me doesn't want to help you. I have thorns in unnatural places, Timas. Unnatural! I will have to go to the healer to remove these thorns. The things I put up with working for you." I glare at him with everything I have as he continues his disgruntled mumbling. "But seeing as you're the King, I suppose it is my duty to help." He stands, trying to pluck the thorns out of his pant leg. "She is a lady's maid to one of the nobles that arrived today. I don't know exactly where she is going, just that her mistress is Lady Dahlia. If I am not mistaken, Lady Dahlia is the daughter of Duke Hemmet, one of the High King's advisors."

"I don't want her working as a lady's maid. She is going to be the Queen of the Day Court! You must go get her and bring her to me."

"I will try, but I think this will take her time to adjust to. She knows nothing about our people or our culture, and who knows if she even knows anything about the spirit bond."

He's right—this is likely very overwhelming to her. Perhaps I should give her a night to digest everything. I turn my gaze pointedly on Milori.

"You will watch her. Make the arrangements so you can watch her all evening and through the night. I don't trust anyone else until I can talk to her tomorrow," I say through clenched teeth.

"Of course, Timas. I truly am happy for you—you deserve happiness." He offers me a sincere grin.

"Thank you, my friend. Now I must attend to this ridiculous dinner for what will surely be the longest night of my life."

Chapter 7

Emilia

B eing a lady's maid is exhausting. After my very strange encounter with the King, I raced all the way back to Lady Dahlia's room. Honestly, I'm not even sure how I got there. By the time I returned, I didn't have time to process anything that had just happened. As expected, Lady Dahlia was yelling at both Sigrid and me to prepare her for dinner. Faster than I knew possible, Sigrid and I had Lady Dahlia dressed and ready. Without a backwards glance, she was out the door, and we tidied up to prepare for her return. Far too soon, she returned, annoyed that the King hadn't even taken notice of her. In fact, he hadn't noticed anyone, according to the Lady, and I took a secret pleasure in this news. After we helped her into bed, I was finally left with a moment to think about my encounter with the King.

He was beautiful, I remember, with long black hair and braids framing his face, with deep blue eyes. Something terrifying lives behind them, but it doesn't scare me like it probably should. He is powerful; you can see that very clearly, but there is also something... something I can't put my finger on. He wore blue silk pants and a blue and white robe that showed much of his bare chest. His chest was covered in swirling markings that seemed to glow lightly. When he touched me, my whole body warmed, and a tugging in my chest took my breath away. I have seen many males, but he was the first to ever elicit such feelings from me. My body craved to be with him, but it was all too much, too quickly. Perhaps he was intoxicated or something, calling me his queen. It had to be some joke. I'm a servant to a Lady. I'm no one of prestige, yet he looked at me like I was the most important person in the world.

But it doesn't matter. It can't matter. I have a job to do, and no amount of attractiveness will pull me away from that.

I barely get a few hours of sleep before I wake up early the following day. Garrick told me to meet him by the docks before dawn, so my next task is sneaking out of the palace. I quietly put on my dress and grab my cloak. It's colder here, likely due to the wind coming off the water. Creeping slightly to the servant quarters' door, I open it and step outside. The last thing I need to do is explain to Sigrid why I'm leaving. No one seemed to be in the halls, so I approached the side door I saw yesterday. Once out in the early morning air, I take a cleansing breath. This sneaking around is taking a toll on my nerves. Besides the normal exhaustion, I think I have had a permanent headache for the past year. A light fog covers the ground as I leave the outside gardens and take the road down to the docks. I have an uneasy feeling, like I am being watched. I know I have taken every precaution, and I am as sure as I can be that no one saw me.

Looking around, I don't see anyone, but the sensation doesn't leave me. I can see the water, and the closer I get, the more the boats come into view. It's rather peaceful down here; the sound of water hits the docks and the birds fly overhead making their morning noises. I wish I could enjoy it more, but my task keeps me focused. Following Garrick's instructions, I came to the end of the dock and found a small warehouse, number 12. I'm tucked beside the building, watching to make sure no one sees me enter, and slip into the open side door. It smells of dust and salt water, with crates stacked on top of each other, filling the space. I weave in between them, looking to see if I can catch a glimpse of Garrick. Just as I make my way to the middle of the warehouse, the floor creaks, and a hand comes out and covers my mouth. I start to kick and reach for my dagger when Garrick whispers in my ear.

"Shh, Em, you're not alone."

My heart is pounding, and now, instead of pushing away, I am clinging to Garrick's arms. He pulls me to the back wall and tucks me in behind him. My hands are shaking uncontrollably with the impending confrontation. Suddenly, the ground starts to shake, and I know this is no ordinary person who has followed me here. I should never have come here, especially when I felt a presence, and now my brother is at risk. Maybe the lack of sleep made me sloppy. Maybe I'm just not cut out for this. Who am I kidding? I know I am not cut out for this. From somewhere in the warehouse, I hear a growling and a voice that should cover me in ice and terrify me, but it doesn't. Still unable to move, I hear a strangely familiar voice call out.

"Let her go, Orc." The quiet command is not something to ignore. The voice has power, and we should rightly be scared if he is the reason the floor shakes.

"You will not get to her without going through me." Garrick snarls. Garrick, my half-Orc brother, is a terrifying sight. He is large and a competent fighter, but I think he would lose this fight. Suddenly, it dawned on me: I heard that voice yesterday, the growl from the garden. The person standing in this warehouse is the King of Day Court. But what is he doing here? If they fight, here and now, they will make a mess of both this warehouse and the cover Garrick and I depend on. Taking a fortifying breath, I step out from around Garrick. In front of us is Timas, the Fae King. His eyes are black with streaks of lightning moving across them, and his black hair seems to be moving by an unknown wind. He is shaking with so much power I can't help but stare at him in awe: he is beautiful. Garrick catches my wrist and starts pulling me back behind him.

"Stay behind me." He practically snarls out the words to me. His muscles are tense, getting ready for the fight of his life, but I can stop this. Timas said yesterday I was his queen. He may be delusional, but I don't think he would hurt me. Something tells me he is here to protect me. Something is telling me to go to him and calm him.

"Brother, please. I know him."

"What?!"

"Trust me, okay?"

He is breathing heavily through his nose, not happy at all that I am walking over to the dangerous Fae male. He grunts in acknowledgement, but I know he will lunge and start to fight when he thinks I am in danger. I walk slowly up to Timas, who is still shaking the ground slightly. He still hasn't looked at me because his vision is locked on Garrick. I am within arms reach of him, but he has not moved or said a word; in fact, it looks like he is trying very hard not to destroy this place. I know that if I touch him, he will calm down, though I don't know how I know that. I raise a shaking hand and walk a bit closer to him, gently placing my hand over one of the many bright-glowing markings that paint his body. A jolt races through my body, and I gasp at the sudden feeling. Without overthinking, I flick my eyes up to look at Timas, who is looking down at me. His breathing is still rapid, but his eyes have returned to normal, a beautiful dark blue. One of his hands comes up to rest on top of mine while the other wraps around my waist to pull me closer. He envelopes me in his arms and leans down to place his forehead on top of my head.

"Are you alright, my flower?" With my face essentially plastered to his chest, I take a deep breath of him, and it instantly calms me to my very soul. I push back a little to look into his striking eyes, wondering how this man can be so handsome.

"I-I'm fine. Please don't hurt my brother."

"Your brother?" He quickly looks up and stares at my brother again, but his brow is furrowed in confusion this time. I am able to move myself beside Timas, but he refuses to let go of my waist. I wave my brother over because now, apparently, I need to make introductions.

"Garrick, this is King Timas of the Day Court. Timas, this is my brother, Garrick."

Timas looks extremely lost, but to my surprise, he bows his head slightly to Garrick, which I hope is a good sign. Garrick still looks like he wants to murder someone, so I walk over to him and stand right in front of him with my back to the King. The King starts emitting his signature growl again, but I need this tension to ease.

"I met him yesterday in the gardens, Garrick. I promise he has done nothing to scare me or cause me harm."

"Emilia, I don't understand why he is here."

"Yes, an excellent question. I don't know why he is here either, so let's ask him." We both turn to look at Timas, who seems to be itching to get closer to me but is holding himself back. Somehow, I find this endearing.

"I was going to ask you both why you are meeting in a warehouse before dawn. Sneaking out of the palace, one might think you are a spy." My heart rate skyrockets at his assessment because I am a spy, but I'm not spying on the Day Court. I grab Garrick's hand, and Timas' eyes go directly to my movement.

"I see. You are a spy, then." Timas looks utterly dejected, and I want to run to him and make him happy. I cannot fathom what possesses me to have this reaction.

"We are not spying on you or the Day Court." I rush out my words, hoping he will listen to us.

"So if you are not spying on me or the Court, who are you spying on?" Garrick is unhappy with this line of questioning, so he takes a step forward to put himself between me and Timas. I don't think that is a good idea. I think the only reason Timas hasn't killed Garrick is because I am standing in front of him. I try to pull Garrick back a bit, but there is no reining in his protective instincts at this moment.

"What do you want, King? There is nothing we can say to you, and if you care at all about my sister, then you will leave us alone."

"I care more about your sister than you know. She is my spirit bond." My mind reels with this revelation. A spirit bond? Surely I misheard him. This doesn't happen to humans. The Fae have spirit bonds, and the Orcs have soul bonds, but humans have no distinct bond to speak of.

"That's impossible! She's human." My thoughts exactly, brother.

"Yes, she is. Which leads me to another question: how is she your sister? You are an Orc."

"Half-Orc," I speak up. They both immediately look at me, and I momentarily regret my choice to contribute.

"He is half-Orc; we share a mother."

"Hmm."

"Hmm? What does that mean? Do you have a problem with your spirit bond having an Orc brother?" Garrick doesn't usually get offended by being an Orc, but he takes me and our family very seriously. Even when I first moved in with him and Father, he never treated me with anything other than love and respect. I was his baby sister from day one, and he has acted as a protector ever since. I remember the time when I was ten, and the Orc girls were harassing me about being human. Garrick immediately came to my defence and ran them off. He said that even though I am not green and good-looking like the Orcs, I am still family and still a part of the Dorgan family. Funny what you value at such a young age. At this point, too many things are not being talked about, and I need answers. I walk closer to Timas, hoping he will see we are not here to cause him or his Court any harm. The last thing we need is to be drawing attention to ourselves.

"Timas, I'm sorry. I can't imagine you can look at this situation and feel like you can trust us, but I promise we have no ill will toward the Fae. We are simply trying to stay alive and save our father."

"Emilia!"

"I think we can trust him, Garrick. I have this sense that I can trust him. I don't know why, but I do."

Garrick curses under his breath as he looks at me.

"You are his spirit bond."

"Um, well, I don't know about that, but I do feel I can trust him." Timas still seems on edge. He moves closer to me with every passing minute.

"My flower, I realise you may not understand what a spirit bond is, but you are, in fact, mine. And right now, I am having a very hard time controlling myself with you so far away. Would you please come closer to me?" He looks like a sad puppy eagerly awaiting my response. How could I not go to him? He holds his arm out to me, and like an invisible string is pulling me, I walk into his outstretched arms. He is so warm and comforting, and I am not sure I ever want to leave his presence. The icy realisation of my circumstances reminds me that that can't happen, and I need to make sure I go back to Lady Dahlia and continue saving my father's life. Timas leans down again and kisses me on top of the head.

"Thank you." It's like he finally took a full breath since the conflict arose.

"Though I don't know the nature of the trouble you face, I can offer you my aid. I believe the palace will be a better environment for that discussion than this dilapidated warehouse...?"

"No, we can't. I must return to Lady Dahlia!"

"My darling, you do not have to work for that disgusting wench any longer. I will take care of you." I snort and laugh at that because though she really is a wench, he doesn't comprehend this circumstance.

"But if I don't go back, she will know something is wrong. If I can't continue to gather the information we need, our father will die."

Timas puts his hand along my face and looks deep into my eyes.

"No, my darling, you do not understand. I am the most powerful Fae in centuries. I have an army at my disposal. I can and will help you. You no longer need to do this on your own." I squeeze my eyes shut, hoping that his words are true. I know I can't make this decision alone, so I glance at Garrick to gauge his response. I trust Timas, but I'm concerned that maybe my head is clouded with whatever is happening with this 'spirit bond' phenomenon. When Garrick meets my gaze, he is standing tall but doesn't seem nervous. With a sombre expression, he simply nods his head as I respond to the King.

"Alright, we will go with you."

"Wonderful. Milori?"

From the side of the warehouse, the same guard from yesterday emerges with a smirk on his face. I didn't even know he was here.

"Your Highness."

"Enough, Milori. Do you have a cloak for Garrick? He will need to walk through the gates to enter the palace. I think it would be best to hide who he is until we are able to address this issue. We will meet you in my suite."

"W-where are we going? Aren't we going to walk with them?"

"No, darling, we are going to fly."

"FLY! Like in the air, fly? With birds?" Milori starts laughing uncontrollably at my panic. He pulls a cloak free and hands it to Garrick.

"I think it would be better if Emilia stayed with me." Garrick's tone is icy.

"Oh, I very much disagree, and truthfully, there is nothing you can do," Timas retorts.

At that moment, Timas picks up my legs, and his large transparent wings explode out of his back. He pulls me into his chest and flies out of the large service window in the warehouse. I screech from the sudden movement and cling tightly to Timas' neck. This is not how I thought visiting the Day Court would go.

Chapter 8

Emilia

The sun is rising and colouring a gorgeous orange and purple sky. The wind beats against my face, sending chills down my spine as I shiver against the cold. I'm holding onto Timas' neck, and I am sure there will be bruises left behind after our trip through the sky. I keep my eyes on the horizon (because I learned my lesson from the sea) and just look out ahead. I don't want to be sick again, especially in Timas' arms. I wouldn't categorise myself as being afraid of heights per se, I'm just, well... fine, I'm scared of heights. The palace comes up quickly, and Timas flies us up to the top of the Northern part of the palace. At the top is a large balcony that takes up more than half the level. Flowers and vines hang from the sides, and large windows decorate the wall behind the balcony. Timas lands softly on the balcony as he descends. My heart is still pounding as he walks us into what I can only assume is his suite.

"Um, I think I can stand now."

"I'm sure you can, but that whole experience has put me on edge, and I don't want to put you down." He pauses before saying, "Sorry."

Tension pulls at me, but I need to look at all the issues I am facing. I am aware of the bonds the other races have, and I have always admired them. I might even go as far as to say I want one myself. Even in our Orc village, I had hoped one day I could have a soul bond with an Orc, though that's hardly applicable now. This may be hard for Timas, but it's not his father whose life is being threatened, it's mine. Timas sits on a very comfy-looking lounge chair with me in his lap, but I just can't sit right now. I push at Timas' arms and pull myself away from him. He is not overly pleased with that, but I need the space. If for no other reason than to think without his physical presence influencing me.

"Look, your Majesty..."

"Timas. I am just Timas to you unless you want to give me a pet name. I have never had one of them before..." His eyes drift away as I realise he is literally contemplating this.

"OK, fine, Timas..."

"So, no pet name," He mutters.

"Timas!" I say with as much force as I can because I am tired, so very tired. "Look, I know a bit about the bond, but you have to understand. This is great and all, but I need to go back to Lady Dahlia. She will be getting up soon, and if I am not there to help Sigrid get her ready, I will lose my job. I can't lose my job."

My hands are shaking, and I am terrified of what might happen if I don't return on time. My anxiety is spiking, yet again, showing me the toll all this has taken on my body. A tear rolls down my cheek as my emotions overwhelm me. How much more information do I need to provide in order to save my father? How do I help protect my brother after leading Timas straight to him? Timas stands slowly and comes to stand in front of me. His hands slide down my arms and hold my trembling hands. The same shock I felt in the garden roars to life as I slowly lean into this man's strong, safe, comforting arms.

"My darling flower, I am sure this whole thing is very overwhelming. But I assure you we can figure all this out... together."

Looking up into his eyes, I see his conviction. I have only ever had my brother to lean on. Occasionally, another Orc has aided us, but it has only ever been us trying to keep Father from being killed by Gormash, the chief of the Northern Orc Clan. But maybe, maybe I can trust him with the truth? No, I need to wait for Garrick. It's not just my life being changed here, it's his, too. I let out a breath and bring my hands to his chest, noting that the markings are no longer burning bright like they were in the warehouse but lightly glowing like they were in the garden.

"I don't know why I trust you so much."

"It's the bond."

"That may be, but I need to wait until Garrick gets here. He is my brother, and I will feel better speaking with him first."

Timas looks hurt. Does he expect me to trust him implicitly? Maybe if I were a Fae, that's how it would work, but I'm not. I'm human. This idea of finding a spirit bond is so unbelievable, but I can't help the doubts that creep into my mind. Despite

Timas' feelings, he nods to me anyway, directing my attention elsewhere.

"Are you hungry? I have a selection of fruits and cheeses that might interest you while we wait for Garrick."

At that moment, my stomach growls, making itself known as I remember that I haven't eaten anything since yesterday afternoon. Even while Lady Dahlia was at her meal, I was worrying about what happened with Timas in the garden and anticipating meeting Garrick this morning. Timas must have good hearing because he doesn't waste time as he goes over to a table laden with fruits, cheese, bread of some kind, and what looks to be a steaming pot of tea. I follow behind him, now drawn in by the delicious smells. Timas pulls out a chair for me to sit on, and that simple act makes my stomach flutter.

Timas grabs an assortment of food and piles it high onto a plate, setting it down in front of me. Without thinking, I begin to devour the food before me. I should be more embarrassed by how much I'm eating or maybe how I'm eating, but I have reached my limit today and just want some food. I'd also give anything for a warm bath, I think to myself but bring my attention back to the present. A steaming cup of tea is placed to the right of my plate, and a waft of peppermint and lemon hits my nose. Gently, I pick up the warm cup and bring it to my lips. Swallowing the hot liquid, I moan with satisfaction. I flick my eyes up to Timas and find him staring at me with unbridled passion. He looks as if me eating and moaning over tea is the most enticing thing he has ever seen, which I highly doubt. He seems to shake off whatever he is thinking and takes the chair right beside mine, scooting it as close as he can to me. I'm not sure what to say, so I just go back to eating my food. Maybe Garrick will get here soon.

"My flower, are you ignoring me?"

Pushing air through my nose, I decide to face this head-on.

"First, I am not ignoring you, I am eating. Second, why do you call me a 'flower'?"

"I call you flower because I found you in the garden." He gently tucks a stray piece of hair behind my ear, and warmth courses through my body. His eyes are so enchanting I can barely look away. What a lovely thing to say, I ponder, realising I really want to like this man—maybe I already do. These bonds don't make any sense. Just as I am about to ask another question, the doors to Timas' suite open, and Milori and Garrick walk in. Standing from the table, I run to Garrick and throw my arms around him. I know Timas said he would come, but a little part of me was scared, especially that I wouldn't see him again. His big arms wrap around me and squeeze me so hard I can hardly breathe, but it feels like home, bringing a strong wave of tears to my eyes. I want to go home, I want to see my father, I want this to be over. I'm so tired. Garrick holds me tight as I let out the emotional weight I have been holding onto for months, the same weight he has likely been carrying as well.

"It's OK, Emmy. We'll be OK." I pull back from Garrick and wipe the tears from my eyes. The snot that is likely falling out of my nose gets unceremoniously deposited onto my dress sleeve.

"Stupid tears." I can't help but mutter.

Turning around to face the Day Court King, I notice that he is no longer across the room by the table but a mere foot away from me, staring at me with deep concern and worry. I feel foolish for breaking down like that, wishing I could have at least tried to hold it together for a little bit longer.

"I'm sorry," I say to no one in particular. Milori hands me a handkerchief from the opposite side of me, and I am suddenly aware of the testosterone that surrounds me. It makes me feel a bit claustrophobic. This situation is getting out of hand. Timas stares at me, questions floating around in his eyes, but I don't have enough time to answer them all right now.

"Garrick, I'm not sure what to do."

Garrick lets out a loud breath, which sounds in equal parts annoyance and resignation. That simple expression tells me all I need to know. He is going to tell Timas our story.

"King Timas, you need to understand this is not an easy situation my sister and I are in... but it is obvious you have a bond with her, and the fates are too strong to fight even if I do wish she had ended up with an Orc." At that, Timas growls deep in his throat, and the floor shakes a bit. I swear Garrick is just antagonising him. Hitting Garrick in the shoulder, I quickly move over to Timas and place my hand on his arm. Last time, touching him worked to calm him down, so hopefully, it will work again. I glare at Garrick because that statement is not helpful, but he smirks and continues anyway.

"We are from the Southern Orc Clans. We lived in a village close to the Northern Clans' borders. Just over a year ago, our village was raided by the Northern Clans, and what we thought was a normal raid turned into a kidnapping. Our family is known throughout the Orc Clans as... unique." That is the biggest understatement. Our family is a laughingstock to many Orcs.

"Everyone knows that I am half human and half-Orc and was raised by my Orc Father. Everyone also knows that when I was sixteen, my good-for-nothing mother came and dropped off my fully-human sister, abandoning her and leaving her in an Orc village." The pain of that memory reverberates through my heart. I remember the bitter wind and the snow beneath my feet as I rushed out of the house, trying to find my mother, who slipped away in the night. Apparently, I am not good at hiding my emotions because Timas pulls me closer to his side.

"We were living in the main Clan areas, but Father felt it would be safer to move away from the larger group and raise Emilia in the smaller village, away from so many eyes. It helped living closer to the mines anyway since Father is a blacksmith, and a very well-respected one at that. It was a good life, and for a long time, no one bothered us; the village had accepted us. But like so much in the Orc lands, peace only lasts for so long. A raiding party from the Northern Clans arrived in the dead of night. Normally, raiding parties come for our resources, occasionally taking prisoners, but it's more about upsetting the balance than anything. This wasn't a normal raiding party, though—the Chief of the Northern Clan himself came. We were all pulled out of the house and Father was dragged in front of Gormash. Father attempted to fight back, but they beat him so badly he could barely move. Despite my efforts, I couldn't get to him."

I can hear in Garrick's voice how much pain that brings him. I know he feels like he failed in some way, even though that's not true. At this point, tears are pouring out of me as I relive that terrible night.

"Gormash brought us back into our house and told us what was going to happen. The Northern Clan had allied with the Human Kingdom to conquer the Southern Clans. The problem was that Gormash knew the High King was going to betray them. He had tried to get a spy into the inner circles before, but was unsuccessful. Not many human nobles hire Orcs, as you can imagine—we are better known for our blacksmith work, not our domestic abilities. Gormash knew of our family and decided Emilia would be a perfect spy, but we were in the warring Southern Clans. His solution was to come in and force us to work for him. Emilia was set up in the Hemmet House to get close to Duke Hemmet, and I am the liaison between Emilia and the scouts watching us. I would receive reports from her and send the information back to Gormash." Garrick's shoulders are tense, and he is obviously struggling to tell Timas our story. Garrick continues.

"If we don't produce enough information, they will continue to torment our father. If we become useless, they will kill him, and we will be exiled from our home. Father can send notes to us, but we haven't seen him in over a year. All we know is he is being held in the main city, serving as a blacksmith to Gormash. His life is used constantly to 'keep us in line.' So Emilia keeping this job is imperative to keeping our father alive." Timas listens to Garrick, his face giving nothing away as to his thoughts. I hope we didn't misplace our trust because if he doesn't help us, well I guess not much will change.

Chapter 9

Timas

I am fuming and trying desperately not to let my anger take control. My precious and beautiful flower has been through so much in her short time in this world. I want to destroy Gormash for the torment he has put her through and the pain he has caused her father. I know that the Orc lands are divided into two regions: the Northern Clans and the Southern Clans, and it sounds as if my spirit bond is from the Southern Clans. My understanding is that they still live in somewhat primitive ways, leaning towards the old ways of Orc life and traditions. Ruk leads the Southern region and is well-respected by his clans.

Meanwhile, the Northern Clans are led by a strong and brutal leader named Gormash. He has pushed his clans into a more 'civilized' era. They have better housing, but the people are not happy, and there is often dissent among the ranks despite having better technology and a supposedly superior way of life.

All I know is I need this woman more than I need my next breath, and I know that if I can't save her father, she will never be mine wholly. I take a cleansing breath and release the anger I so desperately want to unleash on Gormash or a nearby plant.

"Milori, dispatch some scouts to find out exactly where her father is. I want to know everything: where he is being held, who is guarding him, their routines, everything. Report back within a day."

"Yes, Your Majesty." Milori bows and heads quickly out of my suite to do precisely as I said. Though we often joke with each other, he knows when the job needs to be done well and efficiently, and this is one of those times.

Turning to my darling flower, I see her hope spurring to life, but there is still uncertainty, and I desperately wish to make that go away.

"Oh, my darling. I will retrieve your father. Please do not worry any longer about his safety."

"But if you get him out, he can never return to the village. Gormash will hunt us down. Where will that leave us?"

"My darling, your place is here now. I will take care of you and your family. They will be welcome here." She doesn't look as overjoyed as I was hoping. I can't help but feel hurt by her hesitance. I know it will be an adjustment, but I am sure they can learn to adapt.

"But they are Orcs. They... they will not fit in well here." Yes, like she does not fit in well with the Orcs, but she is too good to think so selfishly. I look at Garrick, hoping he sees the wisdom in this plan. He stands unmoving, his face a blank slate. When I am about to give up hope of him saying anything, he speaks in a quiet voice, not to me, but to my precious flower.

"Emmy... maybe that's okay. You have endured much to live in the Orc Clan. Maybe it is time for Father and I to give as you do. The King... he is your spirit bond. I know we talked about this, and maybe you don't feel what he feels, but he would do anything for you. He would die for you. The connection that links you two is beyond anything you can imagine, and for the King, your happiness and safety are directly linked to his very spirit. I know you would do anything for Father and me, but us coming here is the least we can do. Especially if it means you will be safe and our family can be together." I may not have a high opinion of the Orc race, but I have a great deal of respect for this Orc. I dip my head in gratitude as Emilia stands at my side. Emilia lets out a shaky breath and says to Garrick,

"Will Father be mad?"

"Oh, Emmy, no! He has been agonizing over you having to do this. He wishes he had taken you away earlier, moved somewhere safe for all of us, and even suggested going to the Human Kingdom so that you would be safer."

"You never told me."

"What was there to tell? He sent me those messages while you were serving that horrid girl to save his life. It couldn't change anything. But..." Garrick looks at me now.

"Emilia needs to return to Lady Dahlia until Father is rescued." Without warning, my magic lashes out and strikes the wall beside Garrick. NO WAY am I letting her go back to that wretched woman. She isn't to serve someone but to be my Queen, ruling by my side! Emilia screams and crouches on the floor, which effectively calms my powers like a bucket of cold water poured on my head. I just scared her. My inability to control my anger has scared my spirit bond. I feel so foolish, but the bond is pulling so hard on me that it doesn't want me to let her go. You would think after being in this world for two hundred and fifty years, I would have a handle on my emotions. As it would seem, I do not. I have waited so long to be with my spirit bond. The person who would complete my spirit, the person who would be my Queen, standing beside me to serve the Day Court people. She isn't a servant. She is to be served; she is to be Queen. I desperately try to reign in my anger because not only is it frightening her, but doing anything to harm Garrick will not help me win Emilia's heart. A soft hand lands on my arm, and a warmth spreads through me. Looking down, I see those beautiful pale blue eyes staring at me.

"I'm sorry." I all but whisper. Closing my eyes, I take a deep breath to regain my composure.

"It's okay. All of this is a lot to take in. I have meltdowns all the time but, I just don't have, you know, powers to throw around." She looks so endearing, trying to calm me down.

"I wouldn't say it was a meltdown," I say under my breath. She gives me a sweet smile, which somehow calms my turbulent mind.

"Help me understand WHY Emilia has to return to... Lady Dahlia." Garrick wastes no time filling me in.

"If Emilia doesn't return to her position, the other scouts and spies will report back to Gormash. As it stands right now, we know Father is safe if Emilia continues to report on Duke Hemmet's comings and goings. Though she is not able to be at the estate, all we have been told is that Father is safe if Emmy does her job. I'm just the middleman. Emilia's position is the only thing keeping Father from death."

I can't help but be frustrated by this entire situation, but focusing on that won't do Emilia any good.

"Fine... But I will have guards watch you." Emilia blanches at that. "I'll make sure they are not noticed, my flower, but I won't be able to control myself if I don't know you are safe." I gently graze her cheek with the back of my finger. She is perfect.

"Alright."

As hard as it is to see her leave, I am more motivated than ever to sort this out. The idea of two individuals in a spirit bond not coming together immediately to seal their union is unheard of in my culture. Fae who find their spirit bonds immediately arrange for a bonding ceremony, calling on our priestesses to unite them as one forever. It takes a great deal of control not to keep her beside me, to know she is safe, but I need more information. Once I get the report from Milori, I can put a plan together.

A knock sounds on the door. "Enter." The guard from my door comes in.

"What is it?"

"The council has requested an audience." Where is my chamberlain? For a man whose sole job is to deliver messages to me, he has been annoyingly absent.

"I'll be there in a moment." After the guard leaves, I take a minute to look out across the water to the continent. Something stirs in me. I'm frustrated by Emilia's situation, yes, but with the turmoil in my Court, I feel my attention being pulled in every direction. There never seems to be enough time in the day or year to solve everything.

Before long, I walk down the hall leading to the meeting chambers, and one of my scouts comes out from behind to greet me.

"Your Majesty, I have news. There was another murder, this one in the upper city. Woman, unbonded but a daughter to an influential family." My rage resurfaces. Of all the times to have another murder, this is not it. With so many humans running around, this can cause unfathomable problems. We haven't had an incident in nearly three months. "But there is good news, your Majesty. We have finally captured an assassin, the one who killed the woman. He must have been very new to the profession because he wasn't nearly as trained as the others. His act was sloppy, and he left blatant clues that led to where he was found. We have him in the dungeons."

A jolt of joy ricochets through me, giving me a much-needed jump in my step. This is the first time we have had any real leads in this situation. To actually have an assassin alive! Hope begins to rise in me. Maybe the fates have finally allowed us to solve this issue.

"Have the interrogator speak with him. I will be down once I inform the council." I hasten into the meeting chambers. This is an unnecessary meeting, and I know it's only to complain about the human nobles. Before, I was fine entertaining their concerns, but now I have a lead for the murders. I can finally get information on the Night Court.

"Council," I announce as I walk to the head of the table.

Raza'l immediately starts to complain. "Your Majesty, the Human nobles have left the designated areas. This is beyond what is tolerable. They should be confined to their suites when not attending a function." I look at Raza'l in utter disbelief. THIS is what I have been called here for?

"Please do not tell me you asked for a meeting to complain that the humans are what? Roaming the HALLS?"

"Your Majesty, they are everywhere!" His disdain for humans is palpable, but his annoyance flares my anger because now I have a spirit bond, and my precious flower is a human. It feels very much like an attack on her. But I won't tell them, not yet. The floor shakes with my anger, however, and Raza'l's pompous face changes from righteous indignation to fear.

"Wards have been put up to keep the humans in the designated areas. Your clear lack of faith in the Fae responsible for those wards is insulting. They are here to help us solve our problems. If it is too much for you to handle, Raza'l, return to your private island until the spring festival is complete." My anger doesn't subside, but the floor has stopped shaking.

"And seeing as you are all here, I can tell you we have finally caught an assassin from the Night Court. Unfortunately, another Fae died in the process, but they were able to track the murderer down. He is being detained in the dungeons. So if you don't have any other *pressing* issues," I look directly at Raza'l, "I would like to deal with that."

Silence fills the room as the weight of my words hits each person. Fae superiority is not a priority right now. Finding out how to stop the Night Court is. Estola stands and bows deeply to me.

"Apologies, your Majesty. Would you care for assistance with the assassin?" Estola is not only wise but also has a unique power to force her presence into weaker minds. I have never had an issue with Estola, and I am far too powerful for her powers to work on me. But her power is known among the people, and many are terrified by it.

"Yes, please join me. As for the rest of you, if you request an audience again to complain about our human guests, I won't be so civil."

I walk out of the chambers and head to the dungeons. Finally, we can find out something, anything, about what the Night Court has planned... I hope.

Chapter 10

Emilia

The trip from Timas's suite to Lady Dahlia's is easy enough, but not quick enough. The sun has already risen by the time I enter the room Sigrid and I share. Sigrid is just tying off her apron as I close the door, giving me a questioning look.

"Good morning, Sigrid. Did you sleep all right?" Maybe if I pretend nothing is off, she won't ask me about it. Unfortunately, that doesn't happen.

"Where have you been this morning?" I fold my cloak, which gives away that I most definitely went somewhere, and set it on my trunk.

"Oh... I couldn't sleep, so I went for a walk." My most commonly used lie could be a better one, but most of the time, it works. Sigrid is starting to notice a pattern, I'm sure.

"Mmhmm." My palms are sweating, and the anxiety that lives in my stomach makes itself known, but I am intent on keeping my facial features calm to maintain my story.

"You and Ethan have been getting along really well." Is she making a statement or asking a question? Turning to look at her, she has a bit of a smirk on her face.

"Well, I suppose he's nice. We talk sometimes." I swallow hard, trying not to fidget. I'm not even sure why I'm nervous; it's not like I have any interest in Ethan.

"I see how he looks at you... have you been sneaking out to meet him by chance?" I nearly cough and choke on some saliva. I wasn't expecting that accusation. Sigrid just laughs and smiles.

"Come now. I was young once, and I understand the desire to meet someone. You're both around the same age, so it would only make sense that you would connect." A smile creeps onto my face.

"He's nice." I'm not lying. He is nice. I have no interest in him, but if Sigrid thinks I am sneaking off to see him, it's better than sneaking off to see my brother and then stumbling upon the King. Yes, I would prefer 'young love' as the reason for my absences.

"Oh Emilia, you are too sweet. Now come, we need to get to Lady Dahlia's room before she yells at us and throws things again." I wince at the memory. She once sent a vase flying across the room because Sigrid and I were two minutes later than she wanted. It was a lovely vase, too.

"Of course." Sigrid heads out of the room while I shuck off my wet boots and slip on my flats, which are more appropriate for work. I dust off some of the visible dirt; hopefully, Lady Dahlia won't notice. Lady Dahlia's suite is right next to the small room Sigrid and I are staying in, and when I push the heavy wooden door open, I can already hear her yelling and complaining.

"What is this?"

"Tea, my lady." The small Fae woman holding a tray says.

"It does not smell like tea. It smells dreadful." Lady Dahlia pushes the beautiful delicate cup away, nearly toppling it to the ground. The Fae woman's reflexes are quick as she catches the cup before it tips over. Lady Dahlia stands from the small table she was sitting at and stomps into the bathing chamber. Sigrid follows her but nods towards the poor woman, collecting the tea cup and teapot.

"I'm so sorry, she isn't exactly... a morning person." I reach the table and try to help clean up some tea that Lady Dahlia's abrupt exit spilled. What an ungrateful woman. The lovely Fae woman, with her long blonde hair braided in intricate braids, meekly smiles at me.

"It's fine." She tries to cover the nerves I know she is feeling. It's a feeling I know too well.

"No, it's not. She's a terror." The woman seems shocked by my honest response, but her large smile gives way, and a small laugh surfaces.

"I didn't realize that humans were just like us." She finishes putting the items on her tray.

"It's not much different serving human nobles, I'm afraid. Well, other than that, we don't have any powers, but we have annoying nobles who often treat their staff like dirt."

"We do, too."

"What's your name?"

"My name is Laen. What is yours?"

"Emilia. Laen, it's nice to meet you. Does the kitchen have black tea, by any chance? That is the only kind Lady Dahlia will drink."

"Of course. I will fetch it right away."

"You can just knock at the door. I will bring it to her so you don't have to deal with her." She bows her head slightly before thanking me and leaving.

The wardrobe where we hung her dresses yesterday sits slightly ajar, reminding me I should lay out a dress for her.

"I swear if that whimsy weed is still out there, I cannot be held responsible for my actions." Lady Dahlia nearly yells that as she exits the bathing chambers. I'm mortified she would use such a term. Calling a Fae person a whimsy weed is such a derogatory term! I am so glad Laen isn't here. Lady Dahlia is a guest to the KING, and yet she insults the Fae people! Some days, I think I don't know how much more of this I can handle.

"Emilia! The pink dress. The Blossom Celebration is this afternoon, and I want to look delicate and demure to attract the King's attention." My hand grabs the pink dress, but I can't help but squeeze it hard. The very idea that Timas might find Lady Dahlia remotely attractive sends a spike of jealousy through me that feels raw and unnatural. Loosening my grip, I try to lay the dress on her bed delicately. "He can't ignore me for long. Today's event is supposed to be where the Fae find and start their bonds with one another. With any luck, the King will give me a flower, and we can finally stop pretending we aren't interested in each other." She sighs dramatically.

Unbelievable. She can't possibly think the King would be interested in her.

"Why did this event have to take place outside, though? It will be hot and bright, and my allergies will certainly act up. I'm not an outdoors type of woman. That will be the first thing I change when I become Queen. You both will attend today, so wear your nicer outfits. I don't need you embarrassing me. Bring the white umbrella to match; you can hold that while I walk around. Oh, the things I do for love."

So many thoughts. I have so many thoughts. She can't honestly think she can change an ENTIRE race and their customs because she doesn't like them? Her father did her a disservice, allowing her to get whatever she wanted, whenever she wanted.

"Of course, My Lady." Sigrid is always so polite despite the attitude Lady Dahlia gives.

The morning races by, and we spend the entire morning and past mealtime getting Lady Dahlia ready. We barely have enough time to go and change, let alone eat. The Blossom Celebration is being held on the palace grounds; an entire grove of cherry blossom trees is just behind it. I have never seen anything like it before. Large cherry blossom trees create a canopy for us to walk under. White lanterns hang from the branches, and it feels so very magical. Soft music plays, but I can't find the musicians. Fae men and women mingle about, laughing and smiling with one another. Signs covered in vines and white flowers hang from some of the tree branches, some telling you what the games are and some sharing facts about the grove. Out of the corner of my eye, I see a young Fae man walk up to a beautiful Fae woman and bow deeply to her. Her cheeks flush pink as he stands again, a crown of flowers in his hands, and he offers it to her. She clasps her hands in front of her, smiling and nodding. He places it on her head, picks her up, and swings her around. They look so happy. They look in love. My heart aches for that, to find that love. Too bad there are other things to worry about right now.

"EMILIA!" Lady Dahlia whisper-yells. Startled out of my perusal of the area, I face my mistress.

"Sorry, My lady." I didn't mean to ignore her. I was simply overwhelmed with, well, everything. Lady Dahlia huffs and clasps her hands in front of herself.

"I am getting warm. Fan me." She demands. Quickly pulling the lace fan out, I start fanning her as we walk through the grove. We finally make it to the middle of the grove, where gorgeous flowers and vines surround a small square, raised platform. They seem to somehow be a part of the platform, not just placed around it. A hush falls over the people just as I see him, Timas, enter the gathering. Stunning. He is absolutely stunning as his long hair shines in the light. It can't be normal to be that attractive, can it? His blue eyes scan the space, and they stop abruptly on me, piercing me with the intensity of the sun. My heart beats faster, and my cheeks heat. If only I could turn the fan on myself.

Timas stands on the raised platform looking out onto the crowd, his diplomatic smile strategically placed on his face. It looks forced, but that's what's required when you are a King, I suppose.

"Welcome, esteemed guests and kinsmen. Welcome to the Blossom Celebration. Under these cherry blossoms, we come together to celebrate new love. For our guests, this is a time that we, the Fae, seek out our bond. Over the centuries, many Fae men and women have found their bond, and if they are lucky, their spirit bonds." Everyone applauds at that, but Timas's eyes look directly at me. "This is a sacred bond between two souls that we covet."

"Utterly ridiculous. Who could believe in such an unbelievable idea?" Lady Dahlia mutters under her breath. I can't help but subtly glare at her for insulting such a beautiful connection, a connection so deep that merely saying you love someone can't possibly describe the depth of those feelings. It strikes me strongly at that moment that Timas believes I am his spirit bond. I could have that connection, someone who craves to be with you and know you so profoundly that it's all-consuming.

"We invite our guests to enjoy the festivities, and I wish my kinsmen blessings on the pairs that will be created today. As we usher in the new spring, we can celebrate the new life growing this day." The Fae people shout and dance at the end of Timas's speech. Servants wander around with food and drink, distributing it to the partygoers. Lady Dahlia hits my hand down, trying to get me to stop fanning her, and to my shock, I see Timas, the King, heading right toward us. My palms sweat as I hope he isn't coming here to talk to me. How will I explain that to Lady

Dahlia? I step back with Sigrid, as is protocol, to allow Lady Dahlia some privacy.

Timas comes to stand in front of Lady Dahlia, a polite smile across his face.

"Your Majesty! What a beautiful gathering! I adore the natural aesthetic of the party." Lady Dahlia is talking in a high and very fake voice, which wears on the nerves. You can tell how fake she is, but somehow, she thinks men want her to sound dumb and high-pitched. Or maybe that's what the human men want. I don't know.

"Thank you, Lady..." Timas lets it hang there, knowing full well who she is. However, Lady Dahlia takes it in stride, walking closer to him and laying her hand on his arm.

"Lady Dahlia, Duke Hemmet's daughter. Do you not remember? We spoke yesterday at the dinner." My stomach sours at the sight of her touching him, and a completely irrational feeling of wanting to claw her hands off him nearly overwhelms me. What in the world? Timas steps back from her, letting her hand drop in the process. A small part of me is happy about that, but the larger part is enraged that she touched him. My anxiety continues to grow, especially since Lady Dahlia is not deterred. Timas has actually moved in my direction, which should make me happier, but it just doesn't feel close enough.

This time, Lady Dahlia walks up and pushes out her chest, trying to entice Timas's eyes to look down at her dress. I try flexing my hands and digging my nails into my palms to keep from doing anything that will jeopardize my job, but watching all this unfold is hard to endure. Sigrid notices me and comes up closer to me. Under her breath, she whispers, "Are you okay?"

I shake my head slightly because words are too hard to form right now. I can't look at Timas. What if he is enjoying Lady Dahlia's attention? In truth, she is beautiful. It would make sense if he were tempted by that. I can't take it anymore when Lady Dahlia places both hands on Timas's chest. I need to get out of here. Without much thought, I turn and head out of the grove, far away from Lady Dahlia and her filthy hands that are all over Timas, my Timas. I vaguely hear Lady Dahlia ask where I am going, and Sigrid responds that I have suddenly become ill, but I don't really pay attention. I need to get away from this and find somewhere to have a minute alone.

Chapter 11

Emilia

I wander for a while, just trying to clear my head. Being a spy is hard enough, but adding in jealousy makes this job even harder. I can't keep it all straight. Then Timas came out of nowhere, throwing around words like 'coveted connection' and a 'spirit bond.' Of course, I want to explore that, to have such a deep, romantic connection with someone, but is that all it is? A romantic idea? All I have ever really known is the love of my family. I'm loyal to them, which is why this is so difficult. But a potential love that transcends any other connection sounds... well, it sounds perfect. Other than being jealous to the point of wanting to maim someone brutally. I don't feel the connection that Timas seems to feel, but I still feel something pulling at me to be with him, near him.

Frustrated, I kick a rock across the yard. Somehow, I manage to walk myself to the stables. I'm not even sure how I got here. Horses snort and kick at the hay as I walk by their stalls. Horses are such beautiful creatures, strong and majestic. Toward the end of the row of stalls, a chocolate brown horse nods her head up and down. It looks like she is trying to reach the carrots in the bucket across from her stall. Grabbing a carrot, I walk up to her, palm flat with the carrot in the centre, offering it to her. Her big mouth opens, showing large teeth; she pulls at the carrot with her teeth, nearly inhaling the vegetable.

"Are you hungry?" I ask, patting her long, strong neck. I realize talking to a horse likely doesn't bode well for how mentally stable I am, but she knocks her big snout into my face, which makes me laugh. "You are so beautiful, aren't you?" She snorts again as I hand her another carrot.

The sound of hooves hitting the cobblestone echoes as the stable gates open. Quickly turning, I see a familiar figure riding in. The horse comes to a stop, and the rider hops off.

"Anthony, what are you doing here?" I hope the frustration I'm feeling doesn't show on my face.

"Emilia, it's good to see you." He leans in and hugs me. I made a point of socializing with all of Duke Hemmet's messengers. Garrick told me they were the best source of information, and he told me to use my 'girly ways' to connect with them. I felt strange using people like that, but Garrick was right. They always have better information than most of the people in the house.

"Are you okay? I can't believe Duke Hemmet sent Lady Dahlia to the Fae Court." Disgust drips from every word he speaks. Some humans don't like the Fae people. There has been a lot of mistrust between the two races, which is largely related to the isolation the Fae people impose on themselves. A few decades ago, the Human Kingdom was fighting with the Southern Orc Clan, and from what I heard, the High King asked for aid from the Day Court King but was denied. Due to that decision, many human villages were raided, and the death count was high.

"It's not so bad. Everyone has been quite kind since we arrived." I can't help but defend the Fae people. I don't know them, but they have been kind to me.

"Sure, they're kind to your face, but they don't care about anyone but themselves." He grabs my hands, and the feeling of his hands in mine makes my skin crawl. I want to yank them away, but that would look suspicious since I have actively flirted with him. But the sense of wrongness is overwhelming, so I lightly pull my hands out of his.

"Well, you must be tired after travelling for so long. Are you here to deliver a message?" He doesn't notice me taking my hands away because he looks around at the Fae servants with blatant disgust and suspicion.

"Yes, Duke Hemmet sent me out a few days after you left. He had that meeting with the advisors. Something is happening, and he wants Lady Dahlia to extend her stay here. I have a letter for her." This must be about the attack on the Southern Clan. I sense an opportunity and seize it quickly.

"She is currently attending the Blossom Celebration. I can take it to her so you don't have to wander around the palace."

He takes a minute to look around again. Typically, the messengers only give the letter to the intended individual, but I have convinced him to let me deliver it occasionally.

"I suppose it might be easier for you to find her." He rummages through his bag and pulls out an envelope with a green wax seal. "I need a drink. Being here doesn't feel right." I'm getting a little angry at his blatant hate for this place and its people, but before I can say something that will most definitely get me in trouble, he turns and heads out of the stable with his horse. He must have rented one from the docks, though from what I can tell, horses aren't used a lot in the city.

There has to be a place to unseal this letter without Lady Dahlia knowing I did. Tucking the envelope in my apron, I head for the palace. Maybe the kitchen has something that I can use? But that would draw attention to the fact that I'm trying to read a letter that is obviously not mine. Just as I come around the corner of the stables, I run into a solid chest. A gasp escapes me, and I stumble back in surprise. I try to catch my balance with my arms flailing, but two powerful arms wrap around me instead. Panting, trying to catch my breath, I look up into the beautiful blue eyes of the King.

"Timas," I whisper. What is he doing here?

"Flower, what are you doing?" Irrational anger rises in me, and the image of Lady Dahlia touching Timas races to the forefront of my mind. I know it doesn't make sense, but I don't want to touch Timas after Lady Dahlia touched him. I right myself and pull away from his oh-so-strong arms.

"I am looking for fresh air." That comes out more annoyed than I want it to. Timas looks at me with a critical eye.

"And you couldn't find fresh air at the Blossom Celebratio n... in the grove... outside." Clearly, he thinks he is so smart.

"Yes, it was full of pretty flower smells, not fresh air." I really don't know where I am going with this argument.

"And the air in the stables is better? Because of all the manure, I suppose." I throw my hands in the air because I don't know what to say.

"I just needed to go for a walk! Is that acceptable, Your Majesty?" At this point, my voice definitely rises in volume. Timas notices it is attracting attention, so he grabs my hand, which feels entirely too good, and leads me into the palace. He finds a small room off the side of the main entrance filled with books, parchments, and random floating balls. A desk sits at the back of the room, stacked high with more papers and books. Timas closes the door behind us and turns on me. His blue eyes shine just a little bit brighter, taking my breath away. As he walks towards me, I slowly walk backwards. He is a tall man, and even though I am abnormally tall for a woman, I still need to look up at him.

"Wh-what are you doing?" He is powerful, and his strength seeps from him. Surely he wouldn't hurt me, with all the value they put on a spirit bond. I'm relatively sure they can't hurt a spirit bond.

"You know, not many people will raise their voices at me, and those that have no longer breathe. Usually, I get furious when someone thinks they have a right to question me or yell, but you..." My back hits one of the bookshelves that goes all the way to the ceiling. My heart beats faster, and a part of me is scared, but a larger part of me is very much attracted to this gorgeous Fae man in front of me.

"Has Milori never yelled at you?" Just a guess, but it seems Milori might be the only one who could get away with it.

"He tried once. I was young and couldn't control my powers back then, and he has a scar to prove it. But you, my flower... something about your fire brings me a great deal of joy. So, why did you leave the celebration?"

He raises his hand and brushes a loose strand of hair from my face. He is so confusing. Is he mad, or is he attracted to me?

"I just couldn't be there anymore." I feel like a child. It wasn't his fault that Lady Dahlia was making advances toward him, but it still made me so jealous.

"And why is that, my flower?" His thumb gently caresses my bottom lip, causing goosebumps to cover my arms.

"Because..."

"Because?" He arches his eyebrow expectantly.

"Because I didn't like Lady Dahlia touching you! And if I stayed any longer, I would have done something drastic like remove her hands with one of the guards' swords." I can't look at him anymore; the feeling of anger replaces the pull between Timas and me.

"That is a very specific scenario. I like it." Shocked, I shake my head and look back at him. He is smiling, actually smiling at that.

"You... you like that? Do you enjoy people getting hurt or something?" He comes even closer to me, which I didn't think was possible.

"I enjoy knowing that someone giving me too much attention makes you jealous. It lets me know that you are also being affected by the bond. I didn't think it would affect you at all, so I'm glad to see it is." He leans down and places a sweet kiss on my cheek. My cheeks heat because of how gentle and intimate the kiss is. Pull yourself together, Emilia.

Timas takes a step back and gently tugs my arm, leading me to one of the plush chairs that face the desk.

"Now, for my own sanity: that male from the stables, who is he?" Oh dear, did he see that?

"Oh... that was Anthony, one of Duke Hemmet's messengers. He came to deliver a letter to Lady Dahlia."

"Was it imperative for him to touch you?" Well, that answers that.

"Well, no, not really, but well... this is so awkward. I have flirted with him in the past... to get information... I'm not attracted to him or anything, but he always seemed to have more information than anyone else, so I used this," I wave my hand up and down my body, "as a way to get him to tell me more. That sounds horrible!"

Timas sits in the chair beside me, carefully intertwining our hands together.

"It's a good thing for him that you pulled away so quickly, or else he would have had a real reason to hate the Fae people." I do believe that was a threat.

"No need to do that. He's gone now." I practically squeak.

"Indeed, a good thing, too. You may have been jealous of Lady Dahlia's advances, but seeing that nearly killed him and demolished the entire stables. I guess those breathing exercises Milori makes me do are working." He looks annoyed at that, but I can't help but laugh. That reaction makes him seem more human, somehow. He kisses the back of my hand and smiles at me.

"I'm sorry for overreacting. I would like to say that I don't normally do that, that it's only because of the current circumstances that I acted in the way I did, but I confess, I do sometimes overreact." A sense of shame creeps up on me, not that I am ashamed of desiring Timas, just that I couldn't stop long enough to look at the situation.

"I think we all do sometimes. Now, what did he say?"

"Yes, of course. He said that Lady Dahlia was to try to extend her stay here, and that something had happened after the other advisors visited the estate. He also gave me this letter. I was going to try to open it without anyone knowing, but I thought it would look suspicious if I used steam to open it."

I pull the letter out of my apron to show it to him.

"May I see it?" I hand it over, and his hand caresses mine as he takes the envelope.

"A wax seal, very easy to open." With the wave of his hand, the envelope opens, and the seal is perfectly intact.

"How did you do that?" I lean over to look at the seal. He looks at me, smiles, and says, "Magic."

Lucky.

"Let's read it." I take the envelope and pull out the paper.

Darling Dahlia,I hope you are enjoying your time at the Fae court and that they are treating you well. I need to ask that you extend your stay. Things at home have become more problematic. As it were, it is safer for you to be there for the time being. The High King requests we fight on two fronts, requiring many of my men to fight. I have sent your mother away, so now I ask that you stay until I send for you.I also hope you are doing what we talked about. Catching the eye of the King could elevate our family. If not the King, someone of great power in their court would be an acceptable substitute.All my love, darling,Father

"What an arrogant fool, thinking he can even request to stay here longer. This is not the Human Kingdom. We invited our guests for the week, and that is all." Timas is angry, but not me. This information could free Father. I need to speak to Garrick. Quickly, I stand from the chair and put the letter back inside. Unsure of how to close it, I look at Timas again. He waves his hand, and it seals up quickly. What a handy skill. I think that would have made things a lot easier this past year.

"I need to take this to Lady Dahlia and then find Garrick." Timas follows me toward the door, but before I can open it, he touches my shoulder to turn me around.

"My flower, I don't like you having to return to this woman. She is a vile creature, and I know she doesn't treat you right." It's sweet that he cares so much.

"It's alright. Maybe this will be all I need to free Father." His face clearly says that it won't be, but I have to hold out hope because, without hope, life is full of disappointments. Timas exhales loudly before speaking.

"I will have the message delivered to Garrick so you don't need to run around the city looking for him." My stomach clenches in fear. Too many people already know about this.

"No, I will do it." He cups my face with both hands, looking deeply into my eyes.

"I will send Milori to tell Garrick. You are not alone anymore, my flower. Please let me help you." That sounds better. Milori already knows of our circumstances, so that should be fine.

"Alright." He kisses the top of my forehead and drops his hands.

"I know you need to do this, Emilia, but one day, I will free you from this situation. I hope then you will let me show you how much you mean to me." His smile warms me. His attention is addictive, and as much as I want to hope for a future, it's hard to see it. So I say all I can say.

"Okay." Leaving Timas is harder than it was this morning. Something inside me wants to be near him. Like if he was just close enough, my mind would calm, and the jittery feeling would subside. It is very frustrating when I have things to do.

I enter Lady Dahlia's room to find her yelling yet again at Sigrid, but that only lasts a minute once she realizes I have entered, and she turns her ire on me.

"WHERE HAVE YOU BEEN?!" I wince at her bellowing voice.

"I'm sorry, my lady. I was feeling unwell and needed a moment. While I was out, I intercepted Anthony. He has a message for you from your father." The wrath she was about to pour out on me momentarily subsides, and she comes over and grabs the envelope from my hand.

"If you're lucky, I won't fire both of you when we return to my estate. Now get out. I want to be alone."

Sigrid and I bow slightly and exit the room. I really want this day to be over.

Chapter 12

Timas

The air still has a bit of cold to it, but the sweat pouring down my body doesn't seem to care. Milori takes another swing at my head, and I dodge it easily enough. Sparring with Milori helps keep my temper under control most of the time. Spinning, I kick out at him and land a solid hit on his leg. These sessions are more for using up physical energy, not utilising our powers. Doing that would likely land Milori in a grave. That being said, he'd give me a good fight. My power is primarily derived from the force of nature. I can manipulate nature's powerful energies, and my well of power is deeper than most Fae. Each Fae person has a reserve of magic. Some are stronger than others, and typically, those related to the royal families have stronger powers and greater reserves. Milori doesn't like to tell anyone, but his mother comes from the royal line, and because of that, his powers are strong. He is proficient at fire magic. He could burn a place down quickly if he wanted to. A thunk sounds, and pain radiates up the side of my face.

"Come on now, your Majesty, you need to block." He knows how much I hate him calling me that. I throw a weak left punch, and just as Milori goes to duck, I uppercut using my right fist, hitting him square in the face. He stumbles back while I bounce from foot to foot.

"You were supposed to block." I can't help but smirk at him. He spits the blood out and wipes the remnant off with his hand.

"Ha, ha. Good shot. Now, you were going to tell me what you got out of that assassin." Milori wanders over to the side, grabbing two glasses of water.

"You are supposed to be head of the entire guard, and you don't already know?"

"I had other things to do. A couple of the human nobles have been... difficult. They have been coming up with false reports to have my team show up to assess the problem."

"Your team? Or just you?" We both take a long drink before he responds.

"I thought the Fae were handsy, but the human nobles are on another level. They have some sort of fascination with us, and seeing as you keep running away after every speech, they have resorted to the plebeians of the Fae people." I nearly spit the water out of my mouth at that comment. He is nowhere near being considered a plebeian. He is second-in-command. He is the one who handles issues if I can't do it myself. But more than anything, he is my best friend. The man has more power than most in this Court. But for him, this isn't an unusual occurrence. Fae women always seem to vie for his attention. He's laid-back and charming, though his scruffy appearance and tousled hair are often criticised.

"The ladies are after you for your position, you oversized child. Besides, the spring events don't have as much of an appeal as they once did." The largest reason is that I can't have my Emilia with me. That turns my mood rather sour. I hate being apart from her, and the bond constantly reminds me she is not wholly mine yet. I itch absentmindedly at my skin, a feeling that has become an increasingly annoying problem.

"The bond isn't giving you an easy time, I see."

"You could say that." I don't feel this agitated or like I need to get out of my own skin when Emilia is close by.

"So, you wish to know what we found out." Milori nods, grabbing his white linen shirt and throwing it on, leaving the front undone.

"It was a young Orc from the Northern Clans. Unsurprisingly, his list of successful assassinations is nonexistent. This was the first time he had ever killed someone in this manner. The guards found him in the tavern, drinking to forget about what he had done. After he was brought to the dungeons, Estola and I went for a little... discussion, but she was not needed. After he was chained up, he couldn't get the information out quickly enough, but he told us everything he knew. Estola confirmed the information was true and that he was not trying to deceive us or leave information out." Grabbing my robe, I slip it back on. Without the demand for physical exercise, I am getting chilled. "The Night Court has allied with the Northern Clan as far as we can tell. Gormash, the leader of the Northern Clan, sent many spies and assassins by way of the blacksmithing trade.

Something we will now have to be watching. The young Orc doesn't know much other than the delegates from the Night Court came in the dead of night several months ago to meet with Gormash. Presumably, to talk about how they can disrupt the peace in this Court. The young Orc had been coerced into killing someone, anyone. He has been informed if he does not succeed, his return will bring death for him and his family. It seems Gormash likes to force his people to do what he wants using their families as collateral."

It's disgusting to think someone would use their people like that. I know the Orcs are known for their brutish ways, but I never imagined that the more 'advanced' Clan would use such barbaric tactics.

"The young Orc doesn't know much. Because the Northern Clan is going to war and their more skilled fighters are required there, he was likely used as a throwaway to appease the Night Court. I assume this is the war Emilia is trying to obtain information on. There is far too much backstabbing and secret planning going on. Either way, the Orc says that the Night Court sends delegates to the edge of the Shrouded Forest every couple of weeks to get a report. It puts the entire city on edge because, when they come, a dense fog fills the city. The Orc says the spirits are not happy, whatever that means." Milori shifts on the spot, looking thoughtful.

"So there really isn't much new information. There is no reason why they are doing what they are doing, and it seems there is no end in sight."

I push my hand through my hair because I, too, am frustrated.

"Everything the Orc could tell us, we already knew. The Night Court has a new leader about a hundred years younger than me. He is out for blood, apparently, to right old wrongs."

The islands surrounding the continent have always had Fae inhabitants, and at one point, they were occupied by both the Day and Night court people. The Night Court King at the time decided he was dissatisfied with the ways of the Day Court, as the Day Court has always believed in listening to its people and its advisors. On the other hand, the Night Court has always believed in a totalitarian monarch where the King makes all the decisions despite opposition. The fact that some of the Day and Night courts cohabitated and shared islands in some places spurred on greater conflict. Eventually, the Night Court King decided his rule would be better for the entire Fae race, inciting a civil war where many Fae people lost their lives. My grandfather was the King at the time and was the one to exile the Night Court King and his people, officially separating the two courts. From what my father said, it was a mess, and the people struggled to recover for many years.

Since my becoming King, we have enjoyed peace in our lands. However, it is becoming increasingly clear that our recent issues are very likely due to the Night Court's new King.

"I will have my people vet the blacksmith owners and their workers. Though I suspect we should ask Garrick for help. He might know more about who is coming and going."

"I never thought about that, but it's a good idea."

"I'm not just looks, you know." He comes over and slaps me on the shoulder. "You look terrible, you know that?"

"Thanks, that's exactly what I wanted to hear."

"What are friends for?" he says with a stupid grin. I elbow him in the gut, causing him to fold over.

"Yes, such a friend you are." He recovers quickly and starts laughing.

"I think you need to spend some time with Emilia. You're crankier than normal." I turn to look over my shoulder. He's right, I do need to see her.

"Find her and ask her to meet me tonight for the Lantern ceremony."

"Oooh, a romantic night under the stars." He fans himself like an idiot, and I send a crate from the other side of the yard to him.

"AHH!" The guards standing around the training yard look at each other with shocked expressions. They're likely thinking I'm mad, but Milori knows just how to push my buttons.

"Just because you can fling stuff around doesn't mean you should, Timas!" Milori yells as I leave the yard.

With all this deception and the weight of the murders, I just need a moment. Finding Emilia has been wonderful, but I wish I didn't have to deal with these murders. At the same time, I need to prove to her that I'm worth her time, but fate has a way of intervening. Tonight will be perfect. I will woo her and show her that she can take a chance on this bond, and then perhaps the very crawling of my skin will stop. And I imagine if I get another kiss, I will sleep a lot better.

Chapter 13

Emilia

The laundress in the palace does a much better job than at the estate. Perhaps it has to do with magic? Lady Dahlia's dresses are absolutely beautiful. Growing up, I never imagined I would get to see or even feel such wonderful materials. In the village, we had basic and practical fabric. What's the point in a silk dress when you're going to get it dirty within the first hour of being awake?

A loud knock sounds at the door to Lady Dahlia's room. Looking around, I wonder if I am missing something. Lady Dahlia went to have tea with another noblewoman, so I'm alone in the suite putting away her clothes. Another knock on the door propels me forward to answer it. Pulling the heavy door open, I see Milori standing on the other side. Green eyes look down at me as he smiles with that disarming smile. The man probably has a horde of women falling all over themselves to get his attention.

"Good afternoon, Milori. Is everything alright?"

"Absolutely. I am just here to invite you to a private viewing of the lantern ceremony tonight." Inviting me... what? He wouldn't invite me to something like that, knowing I am supposed to be the King's spirit bond. I must have a look on my face because Milori chuckles at me.

"The King is inviting you to a private viewing of the lantern ceremony tonight." Heat rises to my cheeks. Of course, what was I thinking?

"Oh, um... I'm not sure I can get away. Lady Dahlia is attending tonight, and as far as I know, she is not requiring us to attend with her."

"The ceremony is a few hours long; I am sure you can leave once she has departed and return before she returns." Looking back into the suite, I think about his plan. Getting to know Timas better would be nice, but what if she calls on me while I am away?

"I'm not sure." I chew on the inside of my lip, mulling over my choices. Stay here in the suite just in case Lady Dahlia needs me, or watch what is supposed to be a magical sight. Something tugs inside me the moment I think about Timas. I haven't seen him since yesterday, which isn't all that long, but it feels like it's been forever. With all the risks I have taken this year, one more won't hurt. "Alright, yes. Where do I meet him?"

"I will escort you to the King after Lady Dahlia leaves. Does that sound alright?" I smile and nod my head.

"Yes, thank you." After a slight bow, Milori leaves. Excitement bubbles inside me at the prospect of seeing Timas.

The rest of the afternoon goes by quickly. After putting away Lady Dahlia's clothes, she returns to prepare for the lantern ceremony. Sigrid and I have just finished putting away the makeup when someone knocks on the door. My heart skips a beat. I completely forgot Sigrid would be here with me when Milori came to escort me to the King.

"I'll get it." I give Sigrid a tight smile, head to the door, and pull it open a crack. Somehow, I need to leave without Sigrid being suspicious.

"Good evening, Emilia. Are you ready?" Slightly wide-eyed, I look at him and then back in the suite at Sigrid, who is still putting items away.

"Sigrid is here. I can't leave yet." Understanding the situation, Milori nods his head.

"I will wait around the corner. A large tapestry is hanging on the wall, and just behind that is an alcove with a hidden door. Meet me there." Nodding, I close the door and turn back to the room.

"What was that about?" Sigrid looks up at me.

"Oh, one of the Fae servants asked if we needed anything. I asked if we could get another bottle of that wine Lady Dahlia seems to like, seeing as she just finished it." That sounds believable, I think.

"Good idea, though we should have asked for some more towels. I will go in search of some later."

There has to be a way to leave without looking suspicious.

"I saw Ethan today. Maybe you could visit with him while Lady Dahlia's away? I can cover for you."

"Oh," I forgot, Sigrid thinks I have a special relationship with Ethan... which could be useful.

"You work so hard, Emilia, you can't make your whole life about this job. You should go have some fun." Her smile is so genuine and kind, and I feel awful lying to her, but this could be the best opportunity to leave and enjoy an evening with Timas.

"Are you sure?"

"Of course! Go have fun." I walk over to her and wrap her up in a tight hug. She is too good of a woman to be working for a woman like Lady Dahlia, and she has been so kind to me.

"Thank you." I hope she can tell how genuinely grateful I am. One day, I hope to tell her everything. She has been a good friend this past year and deserves to know the truth.

Quickly, I head over to the door to meet Milori in the hall. I think about changing for a brief moment, but if I only have a limited time, I don't want to waste it. Finding the tapestry is easy enough, and just behind it, I find Milori.

"Ready?" I nod because I don't know what else to say.

He leads me through a series of passages, all lit with lights that float from the ceiling. I try looking at how they hang there, but Milori walks quickly, and I don't want to get lost in the labyrinth behind the palace walls. Eventually, we make it to what looks like a stone wall. Milori finds something along the wall, and it swings open, revealing a library. The room isn't all that large, but it is filled to the brim with books and tomes. The walls are covered from the bottom to the top with books, and off to the right is an oversized chair, inviting a reader to lose themselves. I never gave much thought to reading, but this makes me very curious about what is in here.

"The Queen Dowager used to spend a lot of time reading here. She preferred to enjoy a good book rather than socialise with the masses. Now that she is no longer required to stay in the palace, this room is not used as often, but Timas keeps it clean and ready for when she visits."

Looking around again, I can see parts of the space used and worn. It doesn't look run down but rather loved and enjoyed. Exiting the door, we enter a large hallway that looks much like the others in the palace. The sun is already setting, and as it hits the stained glass windows, a rainbow of colours dance on the walls and floors. Everything seems so magical here. Milori leads me to a staircase that spirals up a tall tower. By the time we reach the top, I am out of breath. You'd think I would be able to handle the stairs with how much I run around, but no, I am left gasping for air. Finally, stepping out onto the top of the tower, the horizon takes up the entire view. The sight takes my breath away at how beautiful it is. We must be on top of one of the tallest towers in the palace. Looking across the channel, I can see the Human Kingdom. The great expanse of green land and trees decorates the horizon. The sun colours the sky in purples, pinks, and reds. Utterly distracted by the view, I hadn't realised Timas was standing on the balcony.

"Hello, my flower." Quickly turning, I find Timas standing by a sea of flowers, cushions, and candles. I can't help but gape at the sight. Timas is wearing his usual blue and white royal robes, and his hair is exactly the same, though it sways slightly in the wind.

"Wow, this is incredible." He sweeps his hand out, revealing more of the space. A small table sits just slightly off the ground; it's filled with food—fresh fruit, cakes, cheese, and so much more.

"Come sit." Tentatively, I walk over to the sitting area. I vaguely hear a door closing behind me, but I am overwhelmed by everything I see before me and don't pay attention.

"Did you do this all for me?" Finally sitting on the cushions, I look at Timas, who has taken the seat across from me.

"Of course. What kind of person would I be if I didn't provide for my spirit bond?" Excitement and nervousness twist inside me. Timas makes me feel so special, but it's also scary to think someone could feel so strongly about you without really knowing who you are.

"This looks amazing!" Smoothing down my dress, which looks very out of place, surrounded by these beautiful things, I try to get comfortable on the cushions, which isn't hard. It's like sitting on a cloud... or what I expect a cloud would feel like.

"Can I offer you a drink?"

"Yes, please." He pulls one of the glasses from the middle of the table and fills it with wine. Setting it in front of me, I reach out to try it. A burst of flavour covers my tongue, a sweet drink that doesn't have the burn that most Orc drinks have.

"This tastes amazing!" I look over at Timas, shocked and amazed at how good it tastes.

"I am so glad you like it. This particular wine comes from one of the islands south of this one. The variety of grapes grown there are sweeter than most other places." Nodding, I take another sip, enjoying the flavour.

"You look beautiful, my flower. I am so glad you came tonight." Looking down at my working uniform, I have difficulty believing I am as beautiful as he says. My hair is likely a mess, and I know a light coating of dried sweat covers my body after running around attending Lady Dahlia. But when I look into his eyes, he seems utterly captivated... by me. Heat floods my cheeks, probably making them beat red.

"I like it when you blush." And now they are getting hotter.

"Thank you." Ducking my head, I take another sip. I'll need serious courage to stay here.

"Now, you must be hungry. Let's eat. The lanterns will be flying soon, and I want you to enjoy every moment of it, but after you have a full stomach."

We eat and talk, which is so comfortable that my body relaxes. The tense muscles I have been living with for the past year are finally releasing.

"Don't you need to be at the ceremony?"

"I already gave my speech. The priestesses will take over the ceremony when it becomes dark enough to light the lanterns." He adjusts himself, getting a bit closer to me.

"So tell me, my flower. What was it like growing up in an Orc village?" Taking a deep breath, I look at the nearly dark sky. It's been a long time since I have thought about what my life was like.

"It was hard at first. When my mother left me with my father, I was terrified. Are you sure you want to hear this? It's not exactly happy at the beginning." By this point, Timas has moved much closer to me. His arm is behind me on the cushion, and his leg nearly touches mine. He seems to wrap around me, making me feel comforted and protected. He brushes my face gently.

"I want to know everything about you, Emilia—the good, the bad, and the ugly, though I doubt that last one is possible." I laugh out loud. Despite myself, I can't help but smile. He makes me feel special and beautiful.

"Mother and I lived in near poverty while in the human kingdom. We travelled a lot. Mother could never keep a job, which forced us to move frequently. I never knew my father. Mother said he was useless and not worth our time. I asked about him for a while, but she would get mad and ignore me when I did. Eventually, I stopped asking. One day, Mother said we were going on a big trip to meet my half-brother. At that point, I had no idea I even had a half-brother. The trip was long and took us nearly a week to get to the large settlement named Dorron. I noticed things had started changing after a while. We rode along the dirt roads on carts full of goods. The human villages were filled with wooden or stone homes in squares or rectangles, but the villages we were riding through were circular, with large spikes surrounding some and animal skulls hanging outside. Leather covered some of the windows and doors. It felt like we stepped out of civilisation and into... I don't know, another world? We arrived at this house on the outskirts of the settlement. It wasn't all that big, one large circle with a couple of smaller ones attached to the sides. The front was full of hanging weapons and racks with hides drying. Mother knocked on the post to the side of the opening, and a large man stepped out. He was huge, close to seven feet tall. It was the first time I had ever seen an Orc before." I swallow around the emotion building in my throat because remembering my father hurts.

"He had soft brown eyes, and when he saw my mother, he was shocked. Mother said some things about not knowing where to go, and he invited us inside. Garrick came home from work sometime later. He looked like an Orc to me, except he had my mother's eyes. My eyes. He was mad—he hadn't seen our mother in years and wanted nothing to do with her. I thought he was mad at me. I was a child, though, and didn't know any better. He stormed off and went to his room, leaving me, my mother, and Zornak, my father, in the room. My father was so kind to me. Despite being a giant in my eyes, he spoke to me softly and made a place for me to stay in his room. He slept out by the fire. The next morning I woke early, cold, and realised Mother wasn't in the bed with me. I climbed out of bed and raced to the door, with no shoes on, standing in the fresh snow. I knew she had left. Left me with people I didn't know. I cried for days after that, not eating much and not talking. It was Garrick who finally broke through. He would sit with me in silence every day. He would carve and sew clothing to keep his hands busy. After a few days, he finished this beautiful carving of a swallow bird. He told me swallows live in flocks and support each other to live. They symbolise moving forward and finding happiness. He said they were my flock now and would love and support me. Zornak was proud to have me as his daughter. Though I was initially frightened, he worked hard to show me I could trust him, giving me the space I needed and being there when I needed it, too. As I got older, they became everything to me. At around eight, Father moved us to a small village called Mogd. Too many people wanted to look at the human being raised by an Orc, it was uncomfortable to go out at times. The village wasn't much better in some ways, but eventually, everyone came to know who I was and that I worked just as hard as my brother and father. They came to accept me, some even going so far as to ask to marry me. Father never forced me to do that. I was content to work with him at the blacksmith shop, making me one of the oldest unmarried women in the village. But I didn't mind, and well, you know the rest, really. Father was taken, and I wound up as a terrible spy." Smiling at my little joke, Timas stares at me with an emotion I can't describe.

"You are so brave, my flower. You were dealt a difficult hand and made something beautiful out of it. I am glad you have people in your life who love you." Looking up at the stars that have come out, I think about how true his statement is. I am very loved.

He continues, "Did you know that swallows mate for life? Maybe it's a sign." Turning to look at Timas, he smiles, making me feel warm inside.

"Maybe," I whisper. "Tell me about you. What was it like growing up in a palace?"

"My life seems rather boring compared to yours. My father and mother loved me dearly, giving me every experience imaginable. I was raised in luxury and wealth. I wanted for nothing."

"Why does it sound like you weren't happy?" His words say it was perfect, but his tone says something else: it was missing something.

"I was lonely for a long time. I wasn't exactly the nicest of children. My power comes from the natural phenomena of this world. It is powerful and sometimes tough to control, and as a child, I did not have control, especially if I was angry. My temper would flare, and I would burn down a building or shake the ground so much the windows would shatter. No one really wanted to be friends with me. On top of that, I was the heir to the throne, and many were intimidated by me. Milori was the only one brave enough to talk to me. I was nearly twenty when I met him, which is young for the Fae people. We don't hit maturity until we're closer to one hundred."

Hmm, I didn't know that.

"Milori grew up on one of the smaller islands away from Sonas. His mother fell in love with someone from the lower class and was ostracised by her family. It was pure luck that we even met the day he came to the palace. His mother wanted him to train as a guard, and due to the royal blood pumping through him, he had stronger powers than anyone he knew back on his home island—not to mention wings, which are exclusively for noble houses. He was an oddity in a smaller community of Fae people, so his mother thought he would do better here. I was in the training yard going through a basic routine when he walked through. He commented on my poor form, which led to me challenging him on the spot. The whole thing drew quite a crowd. He kept up with me. We used our powers at one point because I think we were trying to prove we were better and stronger than the other. Of course, I won, but he shocked me enough to make me stop and look at him. He smiled after the fight, said he enjoyed it, and that no one had ever pushed him so hard. After that, we were inseparable. He is the only one who gets away with making sarcastic remarks towards me. I trust him implicitly, which I can't say for many in this court."

Timas brushes a knuckle across my cheek as he looks deep into my eyes. He must feel so alone since he only has one person to confide in.

"That still sounds very lonely. Did you spend time with your parents?"

Timas looks away, thinking for a moment before turning back to me.

"Sometimes. Father was busy running the kingdom, which made spending time with him hard, and Mother liked to be alone. Too many people would overwhelm her. I knew they both loved me and made sure to check in, but it always felt a little distant. They were chosen bonded, meaning they hadn't found their spirit bonds and instead, married for political reasons versus love. They ended up loving each other a lot, but you could tell that a lot of what they did, they did it out of duty. I never wanted that."

My heart beats a little faster, listening to him.

"What did you want?" Timas moves closer to me so I can feel the heat coming off his body.

"I dreamed of the day I would find my spirit bond—the other half of my soul. The stories of the elusive spirit bond were cherished by all, and I knew I would wait for her wherever she was. The desire to have a love so deep you cannot measure it. To have such a profound bond with a single person seemed like the epitome of perfection. I know I am sometimes... difficult to handle, but my spirit bond would be able to balance me where a chosen bond would not. So I waited... for you." I feel light-headed at how ardent he sounds. He waited for me. Where I can only feel a slight pull towards him, he must feel something far more overwhelming. And I'm jealous.

"You are everything I could ever dream of and more. Your bravery and loyalty are inspiring. The strength that lives inside you has helped you survive so much. In time, my hope is you will understand the depth of affection I have for you. It may feel unlikely, but I already feel a deep connection with you. Anytime you leave me, I become very agitated—ask Milori. He will attest to my poor mood." I laugh because it feels good to bring happiness to his life. Truthfully, he has brought joy to mine.

"You bring me a lot of happiness, too. At first, it scared me—this idea that my person was... well... you. I mean, I'm just a human raised by an Orc—what do I know about the Fae people or even being royalty? It's intimidating, really intimidating." His smile is beautiful, reaching all the way to his eyes. Against the backdrop of the night sky, he shines.

"May I kiss you?" I swallow and nod my head. He leans in and places a sweet and tender kiss on my lips. His hand cups my face, and the other rests on my leg. It feels like we are lost in the moment forever, though I know it is only a moment. When he pulls away, he is smiling bigger than before, and my own cheeks hurt with the smile on my face. This is the best night I have ever had.

"I don't want to rush you, my darling Emilia. I plan to show you I am worth trusting and maybe one day loving."

I don't think he will have to work that hard—I think I may already be falling for this powerful Fae King.

"Can I ask you something?" I've been wondering for a while why Timas has all these markings on his body. Sitting this close to him, I can see the faint lines that cover his body, and curiosity wins out.

"Of course." His eyes shine with sincerity.

"Why do you have these tattoos?" He hums and looks at his partially visible chest with intricate patterns.

"They show how powerful a Fae King is. The brighter the tattoos shine when a Fae uses magic, the stronger the power. Only nobility have these markings, and for the most part, they are usually small and only one or two on the chest or back, but for me, it covers my chest, arms, and part of my neck. Part of the reason we know I am so strong is because of these tattoos. No one has had this many in the past several centuries."

Seems a reasonable thing, I guess. "Were you born with them?" He shifts and gets a bit closer to me, which I didn't think was possible.

"Yes, though, they become more pronounced the older we get." Hmm, that's interesting.

"It's just about time for the lanterns to fly. Come lay here so we can watch them sail through the air. We release the lanterns as a symbol of a new life beginning. Each person releases a lantern into the sky, making a wish for the upcoming year. It can be about a good yield of crops, but commonly, it is to find love for those who don't have it and to stay in love with those who have found it. We Fae people are quite romantic." Laying beside him, he turns his head and winks at me. Just over the wall surrounding the balcony, a wave of lanterns rises in the dark sky. Little balls of light in hues of gold and amber shine like small suns. I have never seen something so beautiful. I hold my breath, taking in the sight, afraid that a single inhale will distract me from it all. Soft voices and laughter float in the air from below as the lanterns rise higher and higher, carrying the wishes of the people. I am speechless, watching something so wondrous take place in front of me. Timas sits up and grabs two lanterns I had not seen when I came onto the balcony. Lighting it, he hands me one and softly smiles at me.

"Make a wish." Closing my eyes, I think about what I want and wish for. I wish for my father's safe return, but now I wish for something else. I wish for the love Timas described, a love that cannot be measured, a connection so deep that two people become one. Letting go of my lantern, it flies high in the sky.

We lay back on the comfortable cushions, watching hundreds of lanterns float across the sky. Hours pass, and I lay in his arms, talking and watching. This night will be one I will remember for the rest of my life.

Chapter 14

Emilia

I sleep well for the first time in over a year. Spending an evening relaxing with Timas does something to me. It gives me comfort and peace, but it also gives me a sour feeling in my stomach. I had a wonderful evening being romanced by the King of the Day Court while my father is living in who knows what kind of condition, waiting for me to save him. I shouldn't be entertaining the idea that I can find love when the first man to have loved me is being held captive.

"Good morning, Emilia. How was your night?" Sigrid is already up and nearly dressed as I wipe the sleep from my eyes and climb out of bed.

"It was... wonderful." Grabbing my uniform, I pull it over my head and tie it closed.

"If it was so wonderful, why do you sound so sad about it?"

"It's not that I'm sad, I just... I am thinking about my father. I miss him." She gives me a sad smile. She knows nothing of my family, in large part because I don't talk about it, but she has often comforted me when I was homesick or missing family.

"I'm sorry, dear." She comes over and gives me a warm hug. She has that mothering presence about her, which has always put me at ease. Squeezing back, I relish the feeling of being cared for. Unfortunately, the hug reminds me of the hugs my father would give me, so I try to control the emotion I show when we pull away.

"Now we need to get to Lady Dahlia's room. She is planning on eating breakfast with Lady Jules today."

Quickly, we get ready and head to her room. Lady Dahlia isn't awake by the time we arrive, so we prepare a bath and set out her clothes. Once her tea is dropped off, I bring it over to the side of her bed, where she starts to rouse from her sleep.

"Emilia, where were you yesterday?" As I look towards Sigrid, panic sets in, and I realise I forgot to ask her what excuse she gave Lady Dahlia for my absence last night. Sigrid jumps in before I can answer.

"Emilia wasn't feeling well last night, like I mentioned." Illness again, a familiar alibi at this point.

"I must have eaten something for supper that didn't sit well with me." Lady Dahlia swings her legs out from the bed and walks over to where her white robe hangs.

"This is becoming a recurring problem, Emilia. Twice now, you have vanished due to some illness. You have become extremely unreliable." She walks over to the small sitting area by the large window. Out of habit, I grab the tea and walk it over to the small table beside the chair.

"I beg your forgiveness, my lady. I will try harder to watch what I eat moving forward." My heart is racing. She hasn't often called me out on being late or missing something, but to be fair, I don't normally do it so close together. She stares at me for a long while. I fidget with my apron under her scrutinising gaze.

"I have to wonder if your loyalty lies with the Hemmet house, Emilia." My heart is beating so hard I hear a whooshing in my ear.

"It seems to me that you have often not been where you are supposed to be. You have been late and have become increasingly distracted. How did you come into the service of the Hemmet house, anyway?" My palms are sweating. This is my worst nightmare coming true. Her direct question as to my whereabouts is the first step in her realising I hadn't always been where I was supposed to be.

"My lady, I promise it won't happen again. I am loyal to the Hemmet house, of course."

"You never answered my question, Emilia. Father has said to look out for spies. Are you a spy?" My entire world is crashing down around me. What am I going to do?

"I—I heard about the position through a family friend. When I arrived at the Hemmet household to interview for the position, I was hired, my lady." The bottom of my face feels numb. This is undoubtedly where I will be found out and killed for spying, and I'll never get to see my brother or father again. I may never get to see Timas again.

Lady Dahlia tuts at me, taking me in from head to toe. "You're too pathetic to be a spy, anyway. You barely know how to mend a dress, let alone spy on one of the greatest houses in the Kingdom." Relief floods my system, but the smaller breaths I have been taking make me feel lightheaded.

"That being said, your professionalism and work ethic are unfit for the Hemmet house. I don't know how I didn't see it before, but your tardiness and lack of consideration for my time are unfitting to be my lady's maid. I no longer need your services. Pack your things and head back to wherever it is you came from." She waves her hand, dismissing me. I'm shocked and stuck in place as she walks by me and heads to the bathing room.

I just lost my job. I just lost the one thing that has been keeping my father alive. Tears well up in my eyes and pour over my cheeks. Sigrid runs over and wraps me in her arms as I cry softly into her shoulders.

"Shh shh, dear, you head back to the room. I will be right there. Everything will be okay." She squeezes me one last time as Lady Dahlia yells for her from the bathing room. Utterly numb, I leave the room and head back to the room Sigrid and I have been staying in.

I collapse onto the bed and weep into my pillow. Everything I have been holding on to for the past year spills out. I don't know how much time passes before Sigrid kneels beside me, pushing my hair out of my face and telling me it will be okay.

But she doesn't know—she can't possibly know that this is a death sentence for my father.

"I know this is hard, Emilia, but you're better than this anyway. I have always thought you deserved more than waiting on stuck-up nobles." Finally able to move, I sit up with my feet on the floor and hands holding the edge of the bed. Where am I to go? Taking a deep breath, I pull in as much strength as possible. I need to find Garrick and tell him what happened. He'll know what to do.

"I'll be okay." My voice is raw from crying, but I manage to say it loud enough for Sigrid to hear me.

"I'm so sorry, Emilia. I have a friend in another Duke's house if you need a job. I can send a letter to her, and she can maybe get you an interview for a position there. It won't be a lady's maid position, but it's a job." I smile weakly at her. She has always looked out for me. I'm not sure I can explain to her how much it means to me.

"It's okay, Sigrid. It'll be okay. Thank you so much for being so compassionate with me, treating me with kindness and helping me navigate this job. It means so much to me that you welcomed me into your life. You deserve better than serving nobles, too, Sigrid." Her eyes have become watery, which makes mine water in kind.

"I'm too old to hope for more, but not you. I love you, dear Emilia. Wherever you go, please keep in touch?" She wipes a stray tear from my eye as I nod in agreement. She nods once in return and stands.

"I better get back. Lady Dahlia will likely be done soaking." Then she is gone. Looking around the small room, I figure I should start packing. Then I can go and find Garrick. Someone knocks on the door after I've put only a few items in my bag. On the other side of the door stands Milori, and he doesn't look happy.

"What happened?" he demands. I tremble with nervousness, but I'm also so emotionally drained that I can't seem to care.

"I got fired." The message is delivered with little emotion, not because I don't feel it but because I am so tired I can't seem to cry again. That will probably change the moment I see Garrick. It might even happen when I see Timas, but right now, it's all so overwhelming that my body has shut down.

"I'll kill her." His face contorts with anger. Somehow, that makes me feel a little better—maybe I'm not as alone as I thought I was.

Chapter 15

Timas

I fear these meetings with the council are pointless and a waste of time. I don't remember Father ever saying the meetings were mostly complaints with no real solutions, or perhaps it's just my rule they have issues with. Either way, I need to focus on what's in front of me.

As I turn the corner, one of my scouts approaches me, bowing slightly in preparation to deliver a report.

"Your Majesty, we have information about Zornak Dorgan." I continue walking down the hall as the scout keeps pace with me and updates me on Emilia's father.

"Go on."

"He is being held in the capital city of the Northern Orc Clan, Ezuren. During the day, he is forced to work as a personal blacksmith for the Chief, while at night, he is chained and held in the basement of a fortified building. The city itself is surrounded by a stone wall, and then within that, the Chief resides in a castle-like structure that is also protected by a stone rampart. Getting in will not be easy. From my understanding, Zornak has been given minimal amounts of food—just enough for him to live and work as needed, but not enough to gain strength and potentially fight back."

Stopping in the middle of the hallway, I turn to the scout. What kind of barbaric practice is that? Starving a man and forcing him to work. My heart breaks for Emilia. If she knew this, it would crush her. There must be more to this story because the scout is fidgeting slightly, though he maintains eye contact.

"What is it?"

"While our scout was there trying to ascertain the whereabouts of Zornak, he was approached by a Southern Orc spy. After a short... encounter, the Orc managed to convince the scout to bring him here to talk to you."

I am speechless. One of my scouts led an Orc spy back to Sonas—as if we need more problems.

"Excuse me?"

The scout bows his head slightly. "I'm sorry, Your Majesty. He says that the spy's information could be beneficial to you. To help free Zornak Dorgan."

I try taking deep breaths to calm my rising anger, but it isn't doing its intended job. A scout's job is to collect information and return with it, not to bring a scheming spy back with him. But if he has information on how to save Emilia's father, I need to speak to him despite my feelings on the matter.

"I assume you will be dealing with this scout for his lack of intelligence! Bringing a spy into our city when it is already under attack by the Night Court is beyond foolish!" The vase of flowers shakes off the table with my rising anger and shatters when it hits the floor. "Because if you do not, I will. Now, where is this Orc you speak of?"

The scout before me trembles slightly but is wise enough not to keep me waiting.

"He is waiting in the barracks near the palace gates, Your Majesty. I thought it best not to give him full access to the palace."

"It is comforting to see the stupidity of the other scout wasn't contagious." Taking my leave, I head directly to the forward barracks.

Inside the smaller entrance room sits a hulking Orc wearing leather pants and a loose-fitting cotton top. He stands and bows his head slightly toward me. He looks like any other Orc except his eyes—they are assessing everything around him.

"Your Majesty." I'm surprised an Orc even knows how to address a royal. Their culture is such that, even to their chieftains, they do not bow. Rather, they bang their hand on their chest while grasping their forearms when greeting someone with authority.

"So somehow, you convinced one of my scouts to bring you to my city to talk. How, pray tell, did you manage that?"

"It's not hard to overpower one of you Fae if you have the upper hand. Your scout needs to be more aware of his surroundings. I would think environmental awareness is something you would teach a scout." He says with a smug smile.

"I'll remind you I am no scout and don't need to hide who I am. Continue antagonising me, Orc, and I will put you in your place." My eyes darken as I address the Orc. He doesn't flinch at my threat, but I can tell in his eyes he knows who would win a fight.

"Now, tell me why you are here."

Nodding, he proceeds to explain. "I noticed your scout the first day he arrived. Though it is not necessarily unusual to have a Fae person visit the city, it is odd that a Fae man would ask questions about the Chief. Any informed person would know that, within Ezuren, you don't ask about the Chief unless you want to draw attention."

I will be having a serious conversation with Milori after all of this.

"As much as I appreciate you sharing with me the inadequacies of my people, there must be a reason you are here."

"When I realised you were interested in Dorgan Zornak, it became clear you were interested in his family. Perhaps his daughter, who the Orc people know is human." The mention of Emilia stirs something inside me. I don't like that so many people know of her and potentially want to use her for their own gain.

"I am from the Southern Clans and have been tasked with watching and monitoring the activities of Chief Gormash. Over a year ago, when we heard about the kidnapping of Dorgan Zornak, my Chief knew something bigger than the usual raids was occurring. We are not entirely sure why Chief Gormash kidnapped Dorgan Zornak, just that they had some use for his daughter. From what we can tell, Chief Gormash has allied with the Human King and plans to invade the Southern Clans. As you might know, the Northern Clans live by a different standard than that of the Southern Clans. There has always been a clash between the two chiefs, so it is unsurprising that Chief Gormash wishes to conquer and subdue my people. My Chief, Ruk, wishes to prevent this invasion, which is why he has stationed spies within the city of Ezuren. My Chief wants to know why you are interested in the Orcs and Dorgan Zornak."

"That is none of your business." I stare the Orc down because I am not out to play games.

"I do not mean to offend. My Chief would like to help you. Dorgan Zornak was a great warrior in his younger years, and before taking on the responsibility of his children, he served the Chief with honour. He wishes to show his respect to a great warrior."

Their aid may be useful, seeing as my scout is far more incompetent than I was aware of, but this could put me in a position where I am someday required to assist in Orc affairs. I have no desire to get involved in the problems of the continent... but for Emilia, I would do anything.

"What kind of help are you offering, and what must I do in return?"

"You are astute, Your Majesty. My Chief merely wishes to speak with you to create a potential alliance. In exchange, he will give you access to the spies currently in Ezuren. We know how to get in undetected, the best places to hide, and the best times to sneak in and, say, remove one Dorgan Zornak."

This type of information will make it significantly easier to rescue Emilia's father. Without it, it could take my people weeks to figure out the same information. A meeting in trade for information. This could either go in my favour or that of the Southern Clans Chief.

"I will consider this and send a message informing you of my decision."

The Orc bows again slightly, realising the conversation is ending. "Of course, Your Majesty. I will be in the lower city, likely spending my time at the tavern. I'll wait for your answer."

Turning on my heel, I head back into the palace. I need a strong drink after this morning. I wave to one of the guards following behind me.

"Bring Milori to me. I have an urgent matter to discuss."

"Of course, your Majesty, but he has been unavailable since this morning. He instructed us to handle all matters—he said that he was needed for something important."

Stopping immediately, I turn toward the guard. Milori is always available to me; I am his King. But if he is delegating his roles, something has happened—something has happened to my Emilia.

"Where was he last?"

"In the human nobles' wing, Your Majesty."

Emilia! Quickly, I turn and head towards my suites. Something uneasy settles into my stomach.

"Find him! Immediately!" I shout over my shoulder as I walk. I don't need to look back to know he is doing exactly as I asked.

Pushing open the doors to my suite, relief immediately courses through my body. My precious flower is already standing in the suite. I race over to her and collect her into my arms.

"My flower, what is wrong? What has happened?" Without saying anything, she clings to me tightly and cries into my shoulder. Whoever did this will pay with their life.

Chapter 16

Emilia

"I'll kill her." The warmth that overcomes me is the same feeling I get whenever Garrick stands up for me or Father gives me life advice. Milori barely knows me and wants to fight for me. It really is touching.

"That's not necessary. How did you know something was wrong, anyway?" The thought occurs to me that his being here means he was either watching my movements or someone else was.

"Timas has a guard on you at all times. I was immediately informed when you left Lady Dahlia's room in tears."

How embarrassing! People were watching me have a mental breakdown. Sometimes, I wish I could crawl into a hole and hide. Leaving the door open, I turn and walk into the small space.

"Yes, well, I had a moment of complete panic and devastation, so tears were a necessary companion."

Milori walks in and closes the door behind him.

"Lady Dahlia questioned why I wasn't attending to her last night. Apparently, Sigrid's excuse was insufficient to throw off her suspicion. She started putting together that I wasn't always where I was supposed to be when I served her. I guess it was inevitable that I would lose my job. I'm thankful I haven't been arrested for espionage. But the future of my father is... not promising." Emotion tightens my throat despite the many tears I've cried already. Grabbing a few more articles of clothing, I put them in my bag.

"Timas will not be happy he caused this turn of events." Quickly, I turn around to face him.

"No, this is not his fault. It's mine. I should have stayed where I was. I should have focused on doing my job, not dreaming of what could be." Milori stares at me thoughtfully. It doesn't matter anymore. Everything is ruined, and I don't know how to fix it. I need to speak to Garrick.

"I need to find Garrick. At the very least, he will know where I can stay until we come up with a plan."

"I can see why you would go to Garrick for help first, but... if I may suggest, you should go to Timas first."

"I think Timas has enough going on with the festival and being a King. He doesn't need to be bothered by my issues." Milori makes a sound of disbelief, shaking his head at me. I'm not sure what he expects of me—I've been doing this without much help for a long time.

"You still don't understand. You are not a burden to Timas. You are his entire world. When we find the other half of our spirit, everything in our life pushes us to be intrinsically one. Everything he does from here on out is for you. Every second you are away from him, he thinks of you. Every smile you smile, he memorises. Every laugh you laugh, he captures and plays again in his mind. Finding a spirit bond is coveted because it completes us so fully we can't believe we lived without it. He has an Emilia-shaped hole that you fit perfectly in. Your problems are his problems, just like his will be yours. You will be partners, supporting and loving each other until the end of your lives."

Every word he speaks is filled with so much emotion that it nearly brings me to tears. The longing in Milori's eyes proves that this means more than I initially realised. I don't think I truly understood what it was to have a spirit bond. Timas has shown me kindness and tenderness. He has shown me patience and understanding. All he has ever done is offer to help and be there for me, and I have run away. Maybe Milori is right. I know I can trust Timas—he will help me.

"Besides, if you think you are staying somewhere other than the palace, you have another thing coming. Timas will throw a fit even a small child couldn't compete with." I laugh, breaking the tension in the room. "You think I am joking? Timas once blew up a chair because the chef forgot to put vegetables on his dinner plate. Vegetables. He was going through that health phase, though." He shrugs like that is normal behaviour, but it just makes me laugh harder. I'm bent in half, clutching my stomach at the story's absurdity, but I needed that. I needed a good laugh to push all the sadness away. After finally regaining my composure, I stand up and address the matter at hand.

"Okay Milori, take me to Timas. At some point, I will need to find Garrick, though. But I will speak with Timas first."

Milori grabs my bag and opens the door. Two sentry guards quietly observe the hall from either side of the door. We exit and start walking down the hall, and both guards follow behind us.

"Um, Milori... why are those men following us?" I try to whisper my question, but one of the guards smiles. Because, of course, he heard me.

"They have followed you the entire time. You just never noticed." Shocked, I look back at them. There's nothing particularly eye-catching about them, but you would think I would notice them at some point, right?

"The moment Timas found you, you had a detail watching you to ensure your safety. Honestly, I'm surprised he wasn't lurking around the corner himself, making sure you were well."

For some reason, that makes me feel incredibly special.

"I'm a really terrible spy," I mutter.

"I wasn't going to say it, but..." I look up at him, slightly taken aback, to find he is just smiling down at me, trying to contain his laughter. He's right, it is sort of funny. Shaking my head, I follow Milori through the halls of the palace. Milori leads me to Timas's suite, which is set apart from where the human nobles have been staying. I can't remember much from the last time I was here, as I was frantically trying to return to my duties. Lady Dahlia's wing is nice, but this side seems extravagant. Periodically, there are domes on the ceiling, letting in the sun. It feels otherworldly, the colours that play off the walls and the floor. Vines hang from suspended pots, making the space feel natural as well. I think the walls are somehow covered in gold, too, unless that is paint? Maybe? Large wooden doors, at least the size of two regular doors each, come into view. If I remember correctly, those lead to Timas's suite. Two guards are stationed on either side of the door. Both step up and open them as we get closer.

There is something so calming about being in Timas's space. The doors to the balcony are open, showing a view of the continent. I can't believe I can say, 'I flew in through this window.' My life has certainly taken an interesting turn lately.

"Timas is in a meeting and should be returning soon. Is there anything I can get you?" Milori stands in the middle of the room, observing me from afar. I shake my head and wander around the space.

"May I ask you something, Milori?" He clasps his hands behind his back and prepares himself.

"Of course."

"Was it hard... moving here to the palace? Timas told me you didn't grow up in Sonas. I wonder how different a simple life away from the city is to, well, all of this." In quiet moments, I have often thought about what it would be like if Father ever was saved and I had the freedom to choose Timas. I am no Queen. I barely know what is socially acceptable as a human. I was raised in an Orc clan, not a noble house.

"It was a change, though I wasn't exactly welcome on the small island I lived on. My powers made me stand out, and the further from the city you get, the more judgement there is towards those who don't fit in. The Fae work to live, and sometimes it's a harsh environment. Anyone who seems to have the upper hand in life is ostracised from the community, which is ironic, seeing as my mother was ostracised for falling in love with a 'lowly farmer'." He shifts his feet as he continues to reflect.

"I was lucky to have met Timas the first day I arrived in Sonas. To my ignorance, I insulted him, and we have been friends ever since. I still struggle with courtly intrigue and which fork to use, but it has become a place I consider home. I think time will do that—it will turn something new into something of comfort."

He's right. I felt isolated and alone when I first lived with the Orcs, but it became comfortable over time. It became my home. It was not the place necessarily, but the people that made it a home.

"Thank you." He nods at me in response. Before I can ask another question, the doors fly open to the room, and standing in all his glory is Timas.

"My flower, what is wrong? What has happened?" I thought I had cried all I could, but I was wrong. Seeing the concern etched into his face made me feel it all over again. Within a moment, he was picking me up and wrapping me in his arms. I let go of all the sadness and fear lingering at the surface. I take in his strength to face the situation's realities. His embrace feels safe, and I haven't felt genuinely safe for so long. His hand wraps around my back while the other gently holds my head. He doesn't say anything. He just holds me, which is the best thing he could have done.

"Thank you." I mumble into his shoulder. He rubs a soothing hand up and down my back.

"Anything for you, my flower. Anything."

Pulling back, I wipe a stray tear from my eye. Timas wipes away the other side.

"Now, what happened?" So he patiently listens while I recount the day's happenings.

"I am so sorry, my darling."

"What's done is done, but I don't know what to do next. At some point, Gormash will find out, and we will have to face the fact that... that Father won't survive this." I choke on the last few words because it all feels pointless now.

"Come here." He leads me to the plush lounge chair, which can seat two people. He sits down and pulls me to sit beside him.

"I have gathered some information on where your father is and, as of this morning, I have a contact who can help get us into where he is. Of course I will, no doubt, have to agree to some conditions."

Milori shifts at this new information. I don't think he is aware of this latest development.

"Care to enlighten the group, Timas?" Milori questions.

"Well, had my second in command been available this morning, he would already know, but I appreciate you making Emilia a priority instead. As an aside, one of our scouts is going to need to be retrained or killed for his severe lack of ability to go unnoticed and instead get beaten down by a Southern Orc spy. I expect you to deal with that, Milori."

Milori doesn't say anything, but looks slightly shocked at the information. He simply nods.

"The Orc demanded an audience. It turns out the Southern Orc Chief would like to know how he can help in the rescue of your father, Emilia." The mention of my chief doesn't make sense. I was sure he was aware of what happened, but he didn't reach out to help us or even send people to rescue Father when he had the opportunity. A bubble of anger rises in me.

"My chief is obviously out for something else because there is no way this is out of the goodness of his heart. He never tried to help my father before. The only reason it has changed is because you are interested. I may have been raised among the Orcs, but they are a very self-centred race. So what does he want? Because whatever it is, he has no right to manipulate you." The longer I speak, the more worked up I get. The smile on Timas's face stops me in my tracks.

"What?"

"Are you afraid someone will take advantage of me? Are you worried about me?" I had to stop and think about that. Yes, I am worried about him. In the short time I have known him, I have started to care deeply for him. Part of me is concerned that this is the magical bond, but the other part of me knows that he didn't rely on the bond to show me he cares. He has made an effort to get to know me outside of it.

"I suppose I am, yes..." I contemplate how to remove the smug smile from his face. He may have been fully on board with this, but I certainly wasn't.

"I appreciate your concern, my flower, but I will be fine. This just forces us to act quicker than I was hoping."

A knock sounds on the door, startling me and interrupting our conversation. Milori answers the door, and an angry voice comes from the other side.

"Where is my sister?" Garrick! He follows Milori into the room while Timas and I stand to meet them halfway. Timas has our fingers intertwined, which draws Garrick's eye. A flush of heat covers my cheeks. I don't know why I'm embarrassed. I'm a twenty-five-year-old woman, for goodness' sake. Get it under control, Emilia.

"I've heard you are no longer employed with the Hemmet household." Garrick looks at me, not with anger in his eyes, but with understanding and exhaustion.

"I tried to beg for my job, but she wouldn't listen. There has to be another way to keep Gormash happy and his anger away from Father."

"I think there is." Garrick turns and sees the table full of fruit by the large open windows. He walks over and throws a few grapes into his mouth.

"Really? You're just going to say that and fill your face with food? You Orcs are a special breed." Milori crosses his arms and raises an eyebrow at my brother.

"Unlike your twig figure, this physique requires food, and seeing as I hiked through the whole city today, I think I can take a moment to eat a 'dak' grape." My mouth falls open. What is happening here? Milori may be slimmer in form, but the man looks strong, and I know Garrick can see that.

"Thank you for the compliment. I have been working extra hard at getting the twig build." No, seriously, what is happening? Are they becoming friends? It seems a strange way to become someone's friend, but Garrick is odd, so I see it. Timas jumps in and redirects the conversation.

"So what do you mean? There is another way to appease Gormash?"

Garrick sniffs out the cheese platter on the table as well and grabs a handful, shovelling it into his mouth. He usually doesn't eat like this unless he hasn't had a meal in a day. Something else is going on here.

"Classy," Milori mutters. Garrick stares at him, unflinching, chomping on the cheese.

"Our contact requested a meeting with me last night. I had to walk halfway across this island to meet him."

"Why not take the grove lines?" Milori asks with genuine curiosity. What's a grove line?

"What's a grove line?" Great minds, Garrick.

"It is the system of transportation from the city of Sonas to the smaller villages around the island." Stunned silence falls on us.

"I didn't have to walk?!" Garrick throws his hands up in the air in exasperation. Shaking his head, he grabs another handful of grapes and throws them into his mouth.

"ANYWAY. Our contact informed me your assignment has changed." Garrick continues, addressing me. "Somehow, they got wind of you being the spirit bond to the King of the Day Court. They want you to spy on him." He points at Timas, which makes me stiffen. Garrick is far too relaxed, eating his fill of food while we are in a crisis.

"Why are you so calm, Garrick? Everything has changed! How do we know Gormash will keep to his end of the agreement, and how did Gormash find out about this," I wave my hand between Timas and me, "because I only found out a couple of days ago."

Garrick really looks at me, and for the first time, I think he can tell I am not alright. A headache starts at my temples, making me shut my eyes in frustration.

"Emmy, I'm sorry. I don't mean to act like this doesn't matter because it does. It's obvious you went through a lot this morning, and I'm sure this isn't helping. I'm just... hungry." I roll my eyes at that because he is always hungry.

"I figure this is better anyway. It's obvious you enjoy being around Timas, and this way, you don't have to pretend anymore. Lady Dahlia can clean her own underwear now."

"Wow, so many things are wrong with that sentence. First, I never cleaned her underwear, that was not my job. Second, I refuse to spy on Timas—there has to be another way."

"I like this idea," Timas says way too calm.

"Really? You do?"

"Yes. It means I can finally take care of you, give you all sorts of clothes and jewels, but most importantly, I can be seen with you and tell everyone I have finally found my spirit bond. It means the world to me that you would seek out my help—I only wish to share with you everything I have, as the bonded do."

"But then I'll have to tell them things about you and... and I really don't want to do that." He grabs my free hand, looking down into my eyes.

"I know, my flower, and I love that you care for me, but this will buy us enough time to get into Ezuren and rescue your father. We can finish the Spring festival. I can present you to the Day Court people as my betrothed, and Gormash will be none the wiser. After the festival, we will head to the continent and find your father."

My heart beats faster. I guess I knew he wanted to be bonded to me, but I didn't think I needed to make a decision so quickly—to decide right now.

"But you barely know me. I understand the bond may be driving this, but isn't it a bit, I don't know, soon?" Timas looks over his shoulder at Milori and nods toward the door. Milori, understanding the unspoken words, walks over to Garrick and starts ushering him out of the room. Unsurprisingly, Garrick can carry a lot of food in his arms.

"I know this is hard for you to understand, but for me, you are, and will always be, the only person I want to be with. Yes, our magic finds the perfect person to complete our soul, but it also tells us there will be no other after this. When one of us dies, the other will follow shortly after because we are one. We will commit to each other eternally during the bonding ceremony before the sun. So yes, my darling Emilia, I want to be your bonded, and that won't change tomorrow or one hundred years from now."

"I'll be dead by then," I whisper. He speaks as if this bond will be the same as two Fae finding their spirit bond, but I'm afraid it won't be so simple for us.

"You still do not understand. When we become one through the bonding ceremony, we will share not only this palace and the things within it, but also our lifespan. Or rather, you will take on a Fae lifespan to keep our souls united. There have been some instances in the past of a Fae and human bonding, and though we don't fully understand how the magic works, a spirit-bonded pair will always join their lifespans. This is not the case for chosen bonds."

"Okay," I say, just above a whisper. I'm certain he heard me because he is grinning from ear to ear.

"So you will be my bonded, my darling Emilia? You will tie your life to mine for as long as we live?"

"Yes, Timas, I will become your bonded." Sweeping me into his arms, he pulls me close and kisses me, one hand entwining itself in my hair as the other holds us close. Spinning me around, he seems to come alive. But the voice in the back of my head has doubts. Timas is sure he can save my father, but can he? Is this the right move to openly tell everyone I am the King of the Day Court's spirit bond? What will the Fae people think? Though the moment feels special, this isn't the end of our troubles... and an unsettling feeling tells me it won't be as simple as announcing our betrothal.

Chapter 17

Emilia

Timas shows me to a set of rooms just beside his own. Similar large arched oak doors lead into a grand space. Timas's suite has a few different rooms; however, this one has one large area with a bathing room and walk-in closet attached. It's breathtaking.

"This is for me?" Timas stands behind me as I take everything in.

"Of course, my flower. Everything that is mine is yours." I can't help but snort at that in disbelief.

"Riiiiiight. Timas, that's ridiculous. We have yet to be bonded, and even still, you run a kingdom! I'm just..."

"What, my other half?" It's still so hard to understand. How is he so confident in knowing I am meant to be with him?

"I've said before, my darling, you may not understand right now, but I will prove that I will not change my mind. You are worth more than the stars in the sky, and if I weren't so sure you wouldn't run away, I would bond you right now." His gaze is intense, and he assesses every part of me. It's clear that I am what he wants, but on the inside, I have doubts. He walks up behind me and wraps his arms around my waist. He is at least a head taller than me, so he puts his chin on my head. Why do I feel so protected in his embrace?

Turning back around, I look at the room again. Large arched windows look out on the cherry blossom grove behind the palace. From here, you can see a portion I missed exploring: a waterfall feature that flows into a small pond and finds its home among the trees. The room has a cosy space to sit by a marble fireplace, which must be fantastic during the colder months. But what grabs my attention is the large bed with a sheer canopy above it. It looks like you can fall and melt into the blankets. I have never slept on anything like that before.

"Timas, it's beautiful—I don't know what to say."

"You don't have to say anything. I am just happy to give you the place you deserve. Of course, this will be your personal room after the wedding, but you will be sleeping in our room with me." He kisses the side of my head, which warms me right through. How can I go from feeling protected and safe to this deep desire for him?

"Now, I need to meet with the council. Apparently, they have more to say." Turning around in his arms, I wrap my arms around his waist.

"What's the council?"

"The council is a group of five representatives who help advise me on court issues. They are there to help give a different perspective and help the King with accountability. They don't have any power to change anything for the most part, but have been a respected part of the Day Court monarchy for generations. Unfortunately, they are not happy about the human noble guests, so they have taken to complaining about them... often."

"Hmm... what are they going to think about this?" I wave between the two of us.

"They will be happy to hear I have found my spirit bond, but one or two of them might have a problem with you being human. But you don't need to worry about that. Right now, your job is to rest and relax. You have had a very long and tiring day. I have requested a local dressmaker to stop by to show you some clothing. You need to pick something to wear to the ball tomorrow, where I can finally tell the world I am one hundred percent taken." He leans down, placing his lips on mine. Overwhelmed by the moment, I wrap my arms around his neck and push my hands into his hair. He softly hums in agreement, deepening the kiss further as his hands travel over my back, neck, and shoulders. His caresses melt away the residual anxiety from the day as his hands grasp my waist, holding us together—but eventually, he slows our kiss and pulls away, giving an agitated sigh.

"I do not want to go." He pouts like a child, which makes me laugh out loud. It's sweet that he wants to stay with me. Honestly, I would like him to stay, too. In such a short time, he has become someone I can depend on. But more than that, he has become someone I enjoy being with.

"The sooner you get done, the sooner you can return." I smile up at him, hoping to show him how much I also enjoy his company. He groans, kisses me on the lips softly once more, and turns to leave. But just as he is leaving, I hear him mutter to himself.

"This is going to be a real problem." I have no desire to stop the smile that travels up my lips, still warmed by his.

True to Timas's word, a wonderful older Fae woman shows up at my door with her assistant in tow, holding piles of dresses.

"Hello, my lady. I am here to show you my wares! The King requested my finest fabrics, so I brought most of them. If you want something I don't have, I will gladly make it for you." Her bright smile makes me feel comfortable, but that honorific does not.

"Please, it's just Emilia. Thank you so much for coming to me. Let me help you with those." She tuts and waves her hand, telling me to relax.

"Nonsense, I couldn't in good conscience call you anything other than what you are: a lady, according to the King." She walks into the space and lays out gown after gown on the bed and the armchair, and somehow, some hang from the open doors. They are all beautiful. There is a green one with gold lining and a red one with silver accents. A pink one that has sheer flowing arms, but the one that pulls my attention is the blue one. It is a deep, celestial blue, but if you look at just the right angle, silver sparkles in the sunlight.

"You like this one?" The woman picks up the blue dress from the bed and holds it for me to see.

"It looks amazing." She smiles sweetly at me.

"The royal blue! I'm sure the King will find it pleasing." Ushering me over to the bathing room, she helps me slip it on. The long arms billow with my movement, while the sheer material makes it comfortable and breathable. As I expected, the skirt flows beautifully, like it is floating in the air. I didn't notice before, but the bodice is intricately embroidered with silver thread, and with each slight movement, it shines. It is the most beautiful gown I have ever seen, let alone worn. The material is much softer than anything Lady Dahlia wears. Her gowns are more stiff and, though beautiful, don't seem to be all that comfortable.

"You look beautiful, my lady." Looking in the mirror at her, I can't help but smile at the compliment. I feel like another person. The woman standing in the mirror is not the same woman who roamed across the continent, determined to save her father. She isn't even the woman who enjoyed her quiet, content life in the village. This woman has spent the past year pretending to be someone she is not, hoping for a better day. The dark circles under my eyes are prominent against the beauty of the dress. It feels like I'm pretending, yet again, to be something I am not. I don't know who I am anymore, but Timas seems to see past all of that. Patting down the fabric, I marvel at the hard work that went into making it.

"You are very talented. This is a stunning dress." The older Fae woman tuts again and continues to adjust the skirt fabric.

"Stop it, dear, you'll make me blush. Shall we try another one? Or is this the one you wish to wear to the ball tomorrow?" Twisting in the mirror, I take in another angle of the dress.

"I like this one. I want to wear this one." She smiles and claps her hands together in excitement.

"Let me just take a few measurements and get this adjusted to fit you." She pulls out a bag full of sewing supplies and gets to work.

I was the one adjusting Lady Dahlia's clothes just yesterday. It feels surreal that I am standing in my own suite in a Fae palace, soon to be bonded to the Fae King. I don't deserve to be in this position, and a part of me is saying there will be many who will be upset by it as well, but I need to focus on the present. The sooner the ball begins and ends, the sooner we can rescue my father. That is the most pressing issue right now. Now, to figure out how to dance.

***

Timas briefly stops in last night to eat with me, but he is soon off to deal with more court matters. He stops in briefly again this morning before he is off doing... well, I guess important kingly things. The ball is only a few hours away, and I have been assigned some lady's maids to help me get dressed. One of the women, Sylphina, has been the easiest to be around.

"My lady! You have such beautiful hair! The brown curls complement your beautiful eyes!" She is young, or at least young for a Fae person. She said she was only one hundred eighteen and a half. After I stop gaping at her, she laughs and tells me that was equivalent to a nineteen-year-old human.

"Thank you, Sylphina." Her happy and excited energy has helped the dressing process immensely, but it all still feels odd. I feel alone in a lot of ways. Timas has been gone, and Garrick has been who knows where. I haven't seen Father in well over a year, and the only other person I have felt close to is Sigrid, and I haven't seen her since yesterday.

"My Lady, why are you so sad?" I need to work on not showing my emotions on my face.

"It's not that I'm sad per se. I am just missing a friend and family." Sylphina finishes pulling my hair back and pinning it with silver pins that match my dress perfectly.

"Maybe I can go find them? I know this must be very hard for you; the King said you are not acquainted with Fae customs. I am here to make your life as easy as possible, whatever I can do." Her innocent smile hits me harder than I expected. She has so much life, so much happiness.

"I doubt that, but thank you. I really appreciate you helping me today." Someone knocks on the door, and Sylphina leaves the room to answer it. Walking back into the main room, I see Milori standing at the door. He spots me and bows slightly. The other lady's maid looks shocked at the display. Maybe it's not common to bow. Should I have bowed? I need to ask what to do in these situations.

"Emilia, you look radiant." Milori is such a fun person to be around, and instantly, my self-doubts float away.

"If I recall correctly, the last time you complimented me, an angry animal growled behind a bush." I can't help but raise an eyebrow and try to hide my smile.

"Ah, it did, didn't it? After you left, he flung me into a rose bush. Two of them, actually. I still feel the thorns sometimes when I move, like phantom reminders." He shudders, and I laugh. It feels good to laugh.

"Is Timas coming?" I have missed him today. Now that I don't have work to distract me, I can't help but think about what he is doing and where he might be.

"Not yet, but he has sent me to tell you that he will be here to pick you up for the ball and is looking forward to it. You should have seen him like a little puppy jumping up and down." Another full belly laugh escapes me. I can't imagine Timas, the elegant and handsome man he is, jumping up and down like a puppy, but the imagery is charming. Milori seems to be enjoying poking fun at his best friend's expense, especially when Timas can't do anything about it.

"And if Timas were to hear you giving away his secrets..." Milori just grins.

"He might make me go for another flying lesson, but seeing as I am in my official uniform, let's not tell him." Sylphina has pulled out the gown and is in the middle of laying it out when the smile fades from my face. I have to stand before the entire Day Court and be presented as Timas's spirit bond.

"Sylphina, Ysella, give us a moment." The two women bow to Milori and exit the room. I should feel nervous being alone with a man who is not Timas, but he feels more like a brother than anything else.

"Having a hard time adjusting, are you?" I half laugh and sigh in one breath.

"How can you tell?"

"You wear everything you think on your face. I am seriously surprised you have been a spy for as long as you have." The laugh this time is sad.

"Desperation. It's amazing what you will do for those you love." The chair by the fireplace calls to me, so I sit and look at the intricate tapestry hanging on the wall above it.

"This all feels a little unreal. Like I'll wake up, and it will all be a dream. I can't seem to reconcile the two lives I feel like I'm living. Part of me loves being able to show up to the ball tonight on Timas's arm, showing everyone I am falling... falling for this amazing man, but the other part of me feels like I am betraying my father. While he is held captive, living in who knows what kind of place, I am living in this grand palace with the finest of foods and clothes." Milori takes the seat opposite me and lays his ankle on his knee.

"It's alright to feel conflicted. This isn't exactly a typical ex-perience. But we will get your father back, I promise. Timas will go to the ends of the earth for you."

"And yet I haven't seen him all day." The words leave my mouth, and I know how childish they sound—it's unreasonable to expect him to always be with me. I guess I truly do miss him.

"It seems the bond is having an effect on you. Definitely not as bad as Timas, but still."

"What do you mean?" Worry fills my stomach as concern for Timas fills me.

"Oh, nothing to worry about besides him being extra grumpy, which is saying something for him. He has been itching his arms like crazy. He says when he is not near you, his body feels tight and uncomfortable. That will all subside once you are bonded." My cheeks flush at the thought of being bonded to Timas.

"I suppose I just feel alone. Garrick is somewhere. My father is, well, you know where he is, and I'm alone." Milori looks at me thoughtfully.

"He is very disappointed he can't be with you, and I know anything I say in Timas's defence might sound like how you feel doesn't matter, but it does. Timas has been dealing with another murder in the city, and with the human nobles still around, the council is on edge about the possible ramifications of one of them being targeted. But he can explain all that to you. As for you being lonely, I have an idea."

The doors to my suite open, and Sylphina and Sigrid walk in. Jumping to my feet, I race over to the woman who has become a mother figure to me and wrap her in my arms.

"What are you doing here?" Pulling away but still holding onto her, I wait for her answer.

"Well, it seems that a certain someone is the spirit bond to the King." I didn't know what to say to her, so I decided to just say it.

"I'm sorry I lied to you, Sigrid. There is a lot going on that I haven't been able to tell you, and... I'm just so sorry. I never meant to lie to you." Guilt twists in my chest. She has been nothing but wonderful to me, and all I've done is lie.

"So you didn't see Ethan a couple nights ago... you saw the King?" I nod my head, slightly embarrassed at the truth of it.

"Thank goodness!" she pats her hand on her chest, laughing. I, on the other hand, am confused. "Ethan is a nice boy, and though it might have been a good match, this one is far better." She lightly taps me on the cheek.

"Now it's time to get you ready, yes?" Still in shock, I sputter with my words.

"What are you talking about? Aren't you supposed to be helping Lady Dahlia?" She weaves around me to the bed where the dress is still lying. Turning back to me with a big smile, I can't believe what she says next.

"She is likely running around yelling at someone, but it is not me. This handsome man came to talk to me today and offered me a job for much better pay, and you should see the room he gave me! It has a huge bed! Not as big as this one, but still!" Still slightly confused, I look over at Milori, who is dusting off his jacket, acting like he is the best thing that has happened to us.

"What is she talking about, Milori?" He finishes pretending to dust his jacket and smiles at me.

"Timas anticipated you would be lonely. As I said, he is disappointed he can't be with you himself as often as he would like. He figured you might enjoy having someone you care about around, so he has hired Ms. Sigrid here to be your attendant and confidante. She is not required to do the tasks of a lady's maid, but she is to be here for you. Timas cares about you deeply, Emilia." I'm overwhelmed by how thoughtful he is.

"Thank you," I whisper.

"All Timas. Though I will tell him I told you it was my idea. It will send him spinning! This will be fun."

Milori leaves and closes the door behind him. Turning back to Sigrid, she smiles and holds up the dress.

"Ready?" Nodding, I take a deep breath, preparing myself for the night.

Chapter 18

Emilia

Standing on the balcony looking out over the cherry blossom grove, I finally have a moment alone. The light breeze will likely mess up the hair Sylphina spent way too long on, but it feels nice. I feel him before I hear him. The moment his strong hands touch my hips, a shiver runs down my spine, and I can feel his warm breath as he leans down to kiss my cheek. A swirl of emotion turns in my stomach. How does one tiny gesture make every nerve in my body fire simultaneously? My attraction to this man is all-consuming at times.

"You look beautiful, my flower." Turning around, Timas has his hair half-pulled back and more intricate braids adorn it. His striking blue eyes rove over me, and I can't help but do the same to him. His usual white and blue robes are gone, replaced with dark blue robes with silver accents. It matches my dress.

"We match!" I exclaim as he takes my hand and spins me around, watching the fabric of my dress flow.

"I may have asked the dressmaker what you chose and then requested a matching robe." His playful grin makes me chuckle.

"That's so cute!" He stops spinning me and squints his eyes.

"I am not cute! I am a terrifying King! The only acceptable compliments are strikingly handsome, unbearably gorgeous, or irresistibly attractive." I am sure my cheeks are red by the end of his little spiel, but I'm still smiling despite it.

"Oh yes, so sorry, frightening King. You are, in fact, strikingly, unbearably, irresistibly attractive." I fan myself to emphasise my point, making him chuckle.

"Are you ready to go to the ball?" Though the nerves in my stomach say otherwise, I nod. Timas takes my hand and leads me out of my suite.

We find ourselves in front of another large set of ornate doors. The guards on either side stand quietly, waiting for their cue. Milori comes out of nowhere and stands close to Timas, but he is looking at me.

"Ah, you are absolutely beautiful, Emilia." The same growl from the garden builds in Timas's chest, making me smile. It must entertain Milori because he starts grinning like a child who found candy.

"It is a good thing I am in such a good mood, Milori, or I might have to ruin your nice new uniform." Milori's mouth drops open in mock horror before he gives a rebuttal.

"You ruined the last one! I'm starting to think you don't want to be friends anymore." A very unattractive snort escapes me.

"You two sound like a pair of old women."

"I'm obviously the good-looking one. He can be the grumpy one." Milori turns to face the door while Timas rolls his eyes.

Timas looks at me and says, "You know, encouraging him only makes it worse."

Biting the inside of my lip, I try to restrain my growing smile.

"I like having Emilia around. Makes you a lot more fun." Milori says to the door, but I know he is talking to Timas. Timas turns to Milori at that and scowls in his direction.

"I'm fun!" The slightly raised shout doesn't really help his case, but he is so cute when he gets teased.

"Sure you are, friend." He hits him on the shoulder and nods to the guards. Before Timas can say anything else, the doors open, and the ballroom comes into view. The room is immense. The ceiling is a series of domes covered in multi-coloured glass. A level surrounds a square-shaped dance floor that is sunken into the floor. Sheer fabric hangs from floating tables laden with candles and flowers. Vines grow up the walls and even sway from the ceiling. Curiously, little lights float in the air that blink off and on. Are those fireflies? No matter, it's absolutely magical. The noise in the room quiets as Timas walks into it, and the hand I have wrapped around his arm tightens with anxiety as I take in the number of people filling the space.

"Spring Blessings! As we enjoy our last event of the week, I want to personally thank all the guests who were able to attend the spring festival. We are especially grateful to share our Fae traditions with those of the continent." A polite clap goes up around the room, though the disdain for the humans from some of the Fae is not entirely hidden. "This time is for our people to start fresh after the cold months. Where new life begins, and new love is created! I am beyond pleased to announce, like some of you, I have found a bond—my spirit bond in fact. My darling Emilia is the light of my life, and I am happy to present her as my betrothed this evening! So let us dance to celebrate the fruitful year ahead of us. Enjoy!" The applause is far louder this time, and music starts to play, filling the space.

Many Fae people look at us with large smiles while others stare at me curiously. But the looks of the noble human women could cut like a knife. Their assessing gaze and jealous eyes make me nervous and slightly uneasy. On the far end, I catch sight of Lady Dahlia. I have seen her angry before, but she currently looks beyond enraged. Timas starts to walk in the direction of a tall, elegant woman who looks a bit intimidating. She is wearing a lovely green gown that fits her perfectly, and her sharp, hazel eyes take me in as we approach.

"Estola, I want you to meet Emilia, my spirit bond." Not exactly sure about the customs, I bow slightly towards her. Timas looks shocked, but Estola smiles and takes my elbow, pulling me upright.

"No, no, dear, you are not to bow to others. They bow to you. You will be our Queen, after all." I grimace inwardly at what should have been common knowledge. This is going to be a very, very long night. Timas pulls me closer to him and whispers in my ear.

"I'm sorry, my flower. I didn't prepare you for this evening, did I?" He looks embarrassed by the encounter, but this is all new for both of us—we will be learning as we go along.

"It's alright. I'm sorry about that," Estola speaks up, breaking the moment between us. A welcome and probably wise interruption, seeing as we are in a room full of people.

"King Timas, why don't you make the rounds while I speak with Emilia? Help her understand some of the ways of court." Timas looks reluctant to leave, but he eventually nods his head and kisses me lightly on the lips.

"I trust Estola. I'll be right back." Slightly nervous about being left in the care of a stern-looking Fae woman, I watch as Timas goes off to socialise.

"I don't think I have ever seen the King so happy before. It looks good on him." I walk over to stand beside the table Estola is standing at while she flags down a server to bring me a drink.

"He makes me really happy." Thankfully, my drink arrives quickly, and I take a long sip. The cool liquid soothes my dry throat.

"I suppose the first thing to say is that you do not need to bow to anyone. You are to be bonded to the Day Court King, which makes you rather important." I huff at the comment. Important? Me?

"I see this will take you some time to get used to."

"I'm no one special. I was raised in an Orc village and served in a human noble house—there is nothing important about me."

"Ah, but you forget one thing. You are the King's entire world, which, in turn, makes you significant to the Fae people. The Fae people love the King. He is good and honourable, though some say he is frightening." Looking over at Timas, who is walking among the many attendants, his smile is restrained, which doesn't suit him. He has never terrified me, but his imposing presence may frighten some.

"I'm out of my depth here. You said you could give me some helpful tips?"

"Of course." She smiles kindly at me. "The first thing to know is that there are five council members. Myself, Raza'l—he's rather grumpy, Zilor—he's less grumpy, Aecus—more preoccupied with wine than politics, and Uldor—very old thinking but reasonable." I try to keep track of the obviously important information on the council members.

"The council members all come from noble houses, which elevates them above most. Some houses still hold to the idea that noble birth alone makes them superior to those of the lower class, but some of us are slowly changing that mentality. The Fae have a social hierarchy which many would love to see changed, while others believe it is not strict enough. Your best course of action in dealing with anyone is to see where they stand on those social issues and act accordingly. That is if you want to maintain the status quo. Part of me would love to see you ruffle some feathers." She stops to wink at me while she assesses the room. I find myself overwhelmed by the intricacy of their noble society. Orcs also have a sense of hierarchy, but it is based on how well you fight, and with that conviction, anyone can rise to the top if they are strong enough. I don't know how I feel about navigating the complexities of the Fae people.

"Either way, don't bow to anyone. Tip your head in acknowl-edgement. We are a prideful race and respect those who demand respect. It's our way, I suppose. I think you will be good for our people and especially for our King." Before I can come up with a surely inadequate response, my former mistress, the illustrious Lady Dahlia, inserts herself into our conversation.

"I certainly didn't expect to see my old lady's maid walking in attached to the King. What kind of favours did you have to give to get his attention? As I recall, you have never been that good at speaking with the opposite sex, and your appearance has always been subpar." Lady Jules stands beside her with a smug look, but they don't know who I really am. The last year of holding my tongue has been one of the most challenging feats I have ever endured, but I don't need to hold my tongue any longer. Estola straightens beside me, sensing the tension between us. Instead of looking at me and assessing the truthfulness of Lady Dahlia's claims, she zeros in on the horrible excuse for a human and addresses her directly.

"Ah, Lady Dahlia, it is so good of you to be able to attend this evening. It is my understanding you have recently lost all your staff. It is a tragedy, really, because it is clear you can barely dress yourself. I am sure I can ask some stable hands to attend to you if you need." Her face turns beat red, her anger growing. Instead of addressing Estola, she turns her fury on me.

"How dare you show up here dressed like that! I brought you to this dismal place; without that, you wouldn't have been able to persuade the King to even notice you. I gave you a job! You owe me, you ungrateful swine!" Her voice has risen, drawing the attention of the nearby guests. Insulting the people she is staying with is not a good idea, but insulting people with powers is an even worse idea, and part of me hopes someone will blow her up.

"Your father hired me, not you. You have no power there or here. I am not ashamed of my past. It has made me who I am today, and there is nothing you can say to make me feel embarrassed by it. My suggestion, Lady Dahlia, is to acquire some of the manners you seem to be demanding of me and not insult the entire race of people you are currently in the presence of."

That stops her rant quickly as she turns around to take in the hateful stares from the Fae people. Suddenly, the floor shakes, and Lady Dahlia's face pales. His presence is powerful as he approaches me, radiating warmth. Looking up at Timas, I see his eyes starting to crackle with the power that lives inside of him. I sometimes forget how magnificent he is.

"You humans are ungrateful cretins! How dare you insult my spirit bond! You have no respect for the Fae people or our culture, which is a greater crime than most among our people." His voice causes the pictures on the wall to shake, and even the window panes tremble from his voice. Lady Dahlia has quickly stepped away from us and is cowering behind Lady Jules. Many around us fear Timas, but more than a few angrily stare at Lady Dahlia. The anger coursing through Timas seems to radiate off his body, and I'm afraid he will break something if he doesn't calm down. Stepping in front of Timas, I reach up and bring his face down to look at me. His eyes have nearly gone black, with streaks of lightning crossing them; it takes my breath away how terrifying and powerful it is. Slowly, I place my hand along his cheek, trying to bring him back to me.

"Hey, hey. I'm alright. She's pathetic and only seeking attention—we don't need to give it to her." Taking in deep breaths, he finally starts to relax, his eyes returning to their beautiful blue. "Hi there, handsome." He gives me a small, quick smile, leaning down to kiss me swiftly. But he returns his attention to the woman who has made my last year nearly intolerable.

"You are no longer welcome here. Your blatant disrespect for the future Queen is unacceptable. I will inform the High King that one of his noble houses has brought shame to his kingdom. Guards, escort this woman out of the room and off this island."

A gasp escapes Lady Dahlia as two imposing Fae guards grab her. She struggles and pleads for forgiveness as she is removed from the room, but no one listens to her. Even Lady Jules ignores her pleas and fades into the crowd, thoroughly embarrassed to be associated with her. Timas turns his attention to the crowded room.

"I will make myself clear. Emilia is to be respected at all times. If I so much as hear a whisper against her, it is not her you will deal with, but me. Now, let us not allow such insolence to ruin the celebration. Let's dance." The noise of the event slowly increases, and people start to dance once again. Timas has wrapped his arms around me—tightly, I think—reassuring himself that I am here.

"Are you alright, my flower?" He looks at me with such devotion. How can you not fall for someone who looks at you like you are their very reason for breathing?

"I'm fine. I thought I was handling her well." Smiling up at him, mesmerised by his very presence.

"You were doing amazing, my darling, but I will not have anyone insult the future Queen of the Day Court, let alone my future bonded."

"Funny, that. You pretty much told everyone we were bonded. You also called all humans 'ungrateful cretins.' You do recall I'm human, right?" Laughing at his obvious embarrassment, he leans his forehead against mine, letting out a defeated exhale.

"I am sorry, my flower. I did not intend to be so thoughtless with my words. You are not ungrateful, and if I had my way, we would have already had the bonding ceremony. So in the interim, that was my subconscious surfacing with its desires." I lean up and place a chaste kiss on his lips. "I know. Thank you for defending me. Thank you for caring enough to defend me."

"Always. Now, let's not let her idiocy ruin a beautiful ball. Come, let's dance. Tomorrow we will go to the continent. I am sure it will be long and tiresome, so let us enjoy tonight."

And that's exactly what Timas does. He dances with me the entire night, hardly sparing a glance at anyone else. I become his entire world, and by the end of the night, I know that I am falling in love with the Fae King.

Chapter 19

Timas

We pack up and make it onto the boat early the next morning. The ball the night before was actually enjoyable with Emilia by my side. Usually, it is tedious to attend such functions, but with her wrapped in my arms, swaying to the music, I found it gratifying. Other than that one brief moment when I considered killing a noble human. If I were confident it wouldn't be an issue, I would have immediately killed the woman. In any case, the evening returned to a much more pleasant event once she left. I was informed this morning that she was loaded up and sent off on a less luxurious craft than when she first arrived. I'm also told she was unhappy and threw—what did the guard say?—a fit, whatever that means. I'm unsure what it means, but it sounds humorous, so I was pleased to hear it. Perhaps she will think twice about acting so entitled and self-absorbed, but I doubt it.

This morning, we begin the journey to the continent to rescue my flower's father. I'm not happy about how quickly we need to accomplish this task, but if we wait much longer, I fear Emilia will be put into an awful situation of having to choose between her father and me. I would prefer her not to have to make that decision.

"I think we have everything. The Noble Guard will arrive in a moment." Milori climbs onto the royal vessel set to take us to the continent. Emilia comes over dressed in a long tunic with leather pants underneath. It isn't the finest material I can provide for her, but this is an outfit she would have worn at home, and she prefers it to the long, elegant dresses that currently fill her closet. I need to find some clothing she likes when we return.

"What is the Noble Guard?" Emilia looks at me when she asks the question. It fills me with pride to know that she trusts me to provide the answers she needs.

"The Noble Guard is a specially trained group of noble fighters. The fact that most nobles are able to fly gives them an advantage over many. They are a small group, and specially trained, but they are better at handling smaller assignments such as this. We will fly from where we land on the continent to where we will camp tonight, halfway to the Southern Orc settlement, Dorron."

A loud thunk sounds on the boat floor where Garrick has dropped a reasonably heavy bag.

"And how are the non-flying people supposed to travel with you?" My smile pulls to the side because he won't like how he, in particular, is getting there.

"I will carry Emilia, whereas Milori will carry you."

"Me?!" Milori starts paying attention now. I thought it would be rather humorous to see them paired together. "Have you seen him? He's a giant boulder! I can't carry him!" Milori looks appropriately irritated, transforming my small smile into a proper one.

"Boulder?! I am the perfect specimen of the Orc form. You should be honoured to even look at this physique." Garrick crosses his arms over his chest, showing off his large muscles.

"Well, Milori, seeing as you are the strongest of those coming, you'll have to manage."

"You're kidding, right? You have to be joking." I hold his stare. His face falls, showing his defeat. "Why do I always have to carry the Orc?" he mutters, kicking an invisible rock across the deck.

"Oh, and how many Orcs have you transported? I'm putting my life in the hands of a tiny little Fae. I'm likely to die. Can you even carry more than a sack of potatoes?" At this point, Garrick has turned to face Milori, and Milori looks like he might be itching for a fight. On the other hand, Emilia is quietly laughing behind my arm, making this scene much more enjoyable to watch.

"Listen here, Orc boy. I can carry at least two sacks of potatoes and don't push me or I'll carry you by your feet! I need to find a new job." Milori mumbles the last bit, shoulders slumped as he stomps away to the other side of the boat. Garrick rolls his shoulders and walks to the opposite side of Milori. Emilia wraps her hand around my arm, looking up at me with a smile. Her smile makes me feel like I could conquer the world. I marvel at this beauty that is mine.

"You did that on purpose." There's no sense hiding the humour now. I smile and walk over to the boat's edge, with Emilia holding my arm. We set off, the breeze feeling good on my face and the smell of fresh air and water making me feel free.

"How did your meeting with the council go?" It takes me a moment to answer because I don't want to tell her all the hateful things some of them said about me having a human spirit bond, so I go with a more friendly version.

"They are nervous about our pairing. As far as they know, we are getting to know each other, and in two weeks' time, we will celebrate our future bonding ceremony. My mother will be coming as well. I'm very much looking forward to you meeting her." Emilia smiles softly, but I can tell she's chewing on the inside of her lip. Taking her lower lip between my two fingers, I tug gently so she doesn't injure herself.

"What's the matter, my flower?" She looks back out at the water as the boat moves forward, making small waves in the water. She sighs before responding.

"I don't know. I suppose I'm nervous about a lot of things. Nervous about my father and whether we'll get to him in time. Nervous about what the Fae people really think about their king having a human spirit bond. I'm nervous about all of this being over because it all feels like it's leading up to something bigger, and I don't know if I can handle it."

"My flower, that's entirely too much to keep bottled up inside. I know this doesn't take away any anxiety, but you're not alone, Emilia. Don't hold on to it because you think you have to.

You can give me some to take care of. Part of being your spirit bond means we can weather any storm together. The turmoil inside you doesn't have to stay inside. You can give it to me, and I'll help you carry it." She turns to me, her eyes assessing the genuineness of my statement. Something must click because she leans in and wraps her arms around my waist. I squeeze back, trying not to be too forceful with my own hug. She means the world to me, and if I can show her that, even just a little, I'll be happy.

"Thank you, Timas, for everything." Kissing the top of her head, I rub her back slowly.

"Anything for you, my flower."

The boat ride goes quickly, and a few hours later, we dock on the other side of the channel. The Noble Guard disembarks first as they ready themselves for the short flight. Garrick, Milori, Emilia, and I gather around each other.

"Why can't we fly directly to Dorron?" Emilia says as she adjusts the pack she needs to wear for the trip.

"As delightful as it will be carrying your big lug of a brother for the next few hours, we Fae have a limit to our endurance. Flying on our own would get us closer, but the distance between here and there is still great, meaning we need to rest between flights. I've marked a good place to camp on the map. We shouldn't run into any raiding parties there. The only danger is likely the wildlife, but with his face, I'm sure they'll stay away."

Garrick quietly rumbles his disagreement at Milori while Milori looks ever so pleased with himself. Emilia nods and turns to face me. Everyone gathers around and looks at the map one last time.

"If anyone needs to land for any reason, signal, and we'll do it as one. The priority is to keep a low profile. The fewer people that see the Day Court King flying around, the better, so stay as high as you can without losing oxygen." With the preparatory speech out of the way, I wrap one arm around Emilia's back and another under her legs. Holding her to me feels so right, and the need to pull her tighter to me is strong. I squeeze her just a little to appease that desire. She rests her head on my shoulder, showing her trust in me to keep her safe. My wings unfold out from my back, and with one good pump, we are in the air. Emilia tightens her grip around my neck. I remember our first time in the air. The feeling of her pressed up against my body will be a memory I hold dear for the rest of my life. The flight is long and arduous, and though I've enjoyed holding Emilia tightly for so many hours, I can see the exhaustion setting in on Milori and the Noble Guard. Milori has been holding Garrick at such an odd angle I'm surprised he can still fly. They both looked extremely uncomfortable for most of the trip, except for a couple of times Milori pretended to drop Garrick, which earned him a punch to the shoulder. After the second punch, Milori stops playing that particular game. It doesn't take long to find a good place to land on the side of the mountain. After setting Emilia down, she stretches out the kinks in her neck and legs, which reminds me to do the same with my arms. Having them bent the way I did had caused the muscles to cramp.

"We need to hike for another hour to reach the camping spot I marked. It'll give us a good view of the area and allow us to keep a lookout for anyone who might be in the area." Everyone nods, acknowledging Milori's plan, and we start the ascent up the mountain. Emilia holds my hand, lacing our fingers together as we walk. After a while, Milori and Garrick start arguing with each other.

"After carrying me for that long, you really couldn't get us to the top of the mountain?" Garrick and Milori are just in front of us while the Noble Guard follows behind us.

"Okay, your Orc-ness, when you get wings and the ability to fly, you can choose how far we go. Besides, with all that extra weight on you, a nice walk might do you good." Milori snickers at Garrick, who curls his lip up at him, showing his tusks. "Calm down, Sir Orc-y. I'm just kidding. Your bulkiness makes you look distinguished, like a fancy brick wall."

Milori should have stopped while he was ahead because, before anyone can react, Garrick shoots his hand out, pushing Milori so hard that he goes flying through the air and falls down the mountain. Emilia gasps at the sudden launch of Milori while I watch a familiar sight unfold. Milori catches himself in the air with his wings, righting himself and dusting off his clothes. He flies back up towards us and lands just on the other side of Emilia.

"Is he always that sensitive?" Milori looks down at Emilia as we continue our climb. By this point, Emilia has recovered from her shock and shakes her head with a smile.

"You antagonized him and got what was coming to you." Garrick grunts in agreement, leading the way for our group.

"You're supposed to be on my side! I'm the poor innocent Fae who was brutally attacked by the Orc!" Milori is putting on quite a show now.

"Uh-huh, sure. You're so weak and incapable. That's why you're second in command to the King of the Day Court." She smiles up at him innocently, and he huffs and walks ahead.

"I need to find better friends. I've been thrown off a balcony, a boat, and now a mountain! What is my life coming to?"

The time passes quickly, and we make it to the top of the mountain, where a flat area with limited trees dots the space. The cold wind pushes at our clothing, making Emilia shiver. I pull a cloak out of my pack and wrap it around her tightly. This is going to be a long, cold night.

Chapter 20

Emilia

I pull the cloak tighter around my shoulders as the men fan out to set up the tents and start a fire. Walking to the other side of the mountain, I see the landscape unfolding in front of me. The familiar mountaintops line the horizon. The dips and valleys, filled with trees and flying birds, create a pang of homesickness in my stomach. It has been a long time since I've seen them. Some of the mountains are still covered in snow, and the music of the songbirds is just beginning. It reminds me of simpler days when all we needed to worry about was going to work and coming home. A few twigs crack and break, and looking over my shoulder, I see Garrick approaching me.

"Beautiful sight, isn't it?" Standing beside me, his arm brushes against mine.

"Makes me miss home." Garrick wraps his arm around my shoulder and squeezes me before dropping his arm.

"We'll make it back home." But that's just it. I don't know if I want to go home anymore.

"I wonder where Father is? Is he okay?" A flock of birds forms a group and takes off into the air. The setting sun gives them a majestic backdrop.

"Wherever he is, he's happy you're safe, and he'll be even happier that you've found your bond." Startled by the comment, I look up at Garrick. I've had a quiet fear that Father won't approve of Timas.

"Do you think he'll like Timas?" My stomach twists at the thought of Father disliking Timas and that after rescuing him from his captors, I would still have to choose between him and the man I'm starting to fall in love with. I hadn't realized a tear had slipped from my eye or that this thought weighs so heavily on me until Garrick's thumb wipes my tears away.

"Emmy, if Timas makes you happy, Father will be happy. That's all he's ever wanted for us, to be happy." Garrick wraps me up in a hug and squeezes too hard, like he usually does, making me laugh and nudging his side to give me some space.

"I'd better make sure the tents are put up properly, but I fear Milori will deliberately leave me to the elements if I don't watch him carefully enough." I can't help but laugh at his casualness with Milori. They act more like siblings than strangers who just met over a week ago.

"Be nice," I can't help but say. He gives a half smile and turns to walk away.

The setup for our makeshift camp goes quickly, and before we know it, we're sitting around the fire eating some bread and meat that the palace cook sent along for us. The smell of roasting meat embarrassingly makes my stomach rumble, which everyone but Timas laughs at. He then makes it his personal mission to put as much food into my body as possible.

"Are you sure you've had enough?" For the tenth time, Timas asks me if I'm full.

"Yes, Timas. I've eaten so much I don't even think I can walk after this. That last piece of bread was more than I should have eaten." I smile up at the genuine concern etched on his face. His blue eyes sparkle in the firelight. The sunset, hours before, leaves the cold air that nips at the back of my neck while the fire warms my front. Timas and I stay up while everyone else goes to their sleeping pads. Sitting close together, we watch the fire crackle against the night.

"Come, I want to show you something." Timas stands and holds his hand out to me. Slipping my hand into his, he pulls me from my sitting position. Away from all the tents and the nice warm fire, Timas leads me down a small path, barely lit by the moon above. Into a small grove of trees, there's a clearing entirely covered by fireflies. The scene is far beyond anything I could possibly describe. Everywhere I look, small blinking lights from the fireflies cover the space. The trees are towering, with twinkling lights interlacing through the leaves.

"How is this possible? I've never seen anything like this before." Timas pulls me forward, walking among the insects, leading me straight to a mound of blankets I hadn't noticed.

"I wanted to do something special for you. It's been a hard time for you lately, and I just wanted you to feel the magic I feel when I look at you." The things he says sometimes don't feel real. Still, I can't bring myself to criticize because what woman doesn't want to feel like she means the world to a man, that he would burn it all down to be with her or go against everyone to make sure her father, whom she loves dearly, is rescued and brought back to safety. He leads me to the blankets lying on the ground. They're nothing fancy, which makes sense, considering we have limited space for this trip. As we approach the blankets, the orbs of fire surrounding them become more mesmerizing, and the warmth intensifies. Small spherical orbs give off a subdued light and plenty of heat to stave off the cold.

"How is this possible?" I ask, but I don't know if I'm referring to all the fireflies or the orbs of fire. Timas must understand my surprised reaction because he explains them both.

"The fireflies are a species of the Fae people. They're particularly accommodating when you offer them a place to live in the palace, so when I asked them to help me, they were kind enough to say 'yes' and come here for me. As for the orbs, Milori is adept at fire magic and has placed them here to keep us warm." So much of that needs further explanation.

"Wait! Can you speak to fireflies? And Milori can control fire? Why didn't he do that instead of building a fire at the camp?" We're sitting on the blankets, surrounded by magic I've never seen before. So much of this is so far outside of my understanding that I don't know what to do or say.

"I can't talk to the fireflies, per se. It's more like I can feel them. The connection a King has with the lesser Fae species is unique. Only if you listen will they tell you what they want. As for the orbs of fire, it takes a lot of skill and energy to make them. These will only last for a short while before going out. To create a large fire would expend too much of Milori's energy, but he demanded I not kill you by way of hypothermia, so he insisted on making a few to keep you warm." The whole thing feels so otherworldly. Growing up in this world, we all knew about the magic the Fae possessed, but the vast majority have never seen it for themselves, including me.

"This is something out of a dream," I whisper, still shocked by the beauty surrounding us. Timas pulls me further down so we can lie on our backs looking up at the stars. He grabs some blankets and lays them over the top of both of us. The longer I'm with Timas, the stronger I feel a pull towards him, as if this invisible string ties us together. At first, the string that connected us was thin, barely there, but the more time I spend with him, the stronger it gets. At this point, I'm not sure I can walk away from it, not that I would want to. The crickets chirp while we stare at the moon, curled up in each other's arms.

"My mother would tell me of the times my father would take her stargazing. She said it felt like staring at an entirely new world with endless possibilities." Timas says wistfully.

"She sounds like an amazing woman." Timas rubs my arm lightly with his fingers, soothing me into a tranquil state.

"She always lived in a story she loves to read. My father had special rooms all over the palace where my mother could sneak off and escape into a book when court life became too much.

They may have had a chosen bond, but they grew to love each other fiercely. When my father was assassinated over a year ago, my mother just completely shut down. She never really wanted to be Queen, but she did it out of duty to her people and her King." That breaks my heart a little, hearing how difficult it must have been for his mother, but how sweet it was that his father created safe spaces just for her.

"Can I be honest?" I try to keep the fear out of my voice.

"Of course you can." Snuggling closer to him, I take a deep breath before sharing my fears.

"I'm afraid your people aren't going to accept me, but I'm even more afraid that your mother won't either. Not having a mother figure for most of my life and a terrible one at the beginning of it, I wish for someone who might see me, accept me for who I am, and love me, even if it's hard. Maybe it's an unrealistic hope to have for your mother, but I really want to have a mother. Is that silly? A twenty-five-year-old woman, hoping to have a mother figure in her life." Timas shifts us around so he can look at my face. Thankfully, I don't see the pity, which is what I was expecting, but I see understanding.

"It's not unreasonable to want to be loved unconditionally by a parent. Your mother made a terrible choice in leaving you, but I can say, with absolute certainty, that my mother will be overjoyed to have a daughter. She often mentioned how I would have been easier to deal with if I were a girl. She plans to be here to celebrate our betrothal and sounds very excited to meet you. I think you'll give her the joy she's lacked this past year. I can't, however, prevent her from making some comments about children. The Fae people are notorious for hounding newly bonded couples about children." I know my cheeks are going beet red at the mention of having children, not because they're something to be embarrassed about, but because it all feels like it's going really fast. We meet one day, and the next, we're planning to bond with one another. An image of my father comes to mind, which immediately pours cold water on my emotions because I never imagined starting a relationship without him having at least met the person. And, as it stands right now, he's still locked up somewhere as a way to keep me in line, and the thought sobers me.

"If anything, I should be nervous about meeting your father. He sounds like a formidable and respectable man, and I can only hope he'll see me as a worthy pairing for you." And because my body and mind don't know what to do, I get butterflies and become that much more attracted to him.

"He's going to adore you. You've protected Garrick and me, and he's always valued the sacred bond between races. When I was around sixteen, he told me about the spirit bonds of the Fae people and the soul bonds of the Orc people. I was jealous at the time, thinking that would never happen to me because of the way he talked about it, like it was some untouchable connection that only the gods granted. For the Orcs, the soul bond is apparently to make good, strong pairings to bolster the Orc people, at least, that's what my father said about why the goddess created it. Still, he never really knew how the spirit bond worked, other than to assume it was as strong a connection for the Fae as it was for the Orcs. But sixteen-year-old me dreamed of having one, though experiencing one in real life is scary."

"Are you scared of me, my flower?"

"No, no. I'm not scared of you, but a small part of me is scared of a connection so deep I'll forget everything else, family or myself."

"Being in love doesn't mean you lose yourself or those you hold dear, or at least it shouldn't. It should mean you share the deepest part of yourself with someone who can see you for you, to have someone to laugh with when life is stressful and someone to cry with when pain occurs. My mother often said that, over the years of her relationship with my father, there were times when he needed to hold the weight of the relationship, and then other times she would. They were partners in everything. I cannot promise I'll be easy to deal with. In fact, I can guarantee I'll be a complete beast to deal with at times, but be patient with me, and we'll live this life together."

He paints a beautiful picture, a life I'm now craving. I can see it now: him waking up in the morning and sitting with me eating breakfast or talking through another proposal from the council, me being an ear for him to express his thoughts with no fear of judgment or repercussion. It sounds marvellous. It's then I realize I want that and that I would fight for it if I had to.

"That sounds beautiful." His lips meet mine, and as he moves, I match his movements. The hands that carry so much power turn to the gentlest caresses as he strokes my jaw and neck, drawing me deeper into the kiss. I whimper at the pressure of his body against mine, and a deep groan from his chest matches my call. I'm overwhelmed by the emotion of being desired by such a powerful man. Eventually, we pull away as he rests his forehead against mine, my body flushed by our kiss.

"The bonding ceremony cannot happen soon enough," he grumbles. I chuckle at his comment. He lies back, and I lay my head on his chest. We look up at the stars and talk late into the night. Before I know it, my eyes grow heavy, and I fall asleep in the arms of the Day Court King.

Chapter 21

Timas

The morning sun beats down on my tent and, through the thin fabric, wakes me from a peaceful sleep. After Emilia falls asleep, I hold her in my arms for a long while. I don't want her to get cold, so I pick her up in my arms and walk back to camp. I look forward to the day that I'll hold her in my arms all night, every night. Just as I'm reflecting on such a great evening, I hear a high-pitched scream coming from outside the tent.

Jumping to my feet, I quickly throw off my blankets and exit the tent to find Milori dancing around, shaking out his clothes and running away from his tent.

"What the FAIRY RING is that?!" Looking around, the Noble Guard is just standing around, chuckling at their commander while Garrick is on the ground, holding his stomach and laughing. The adrenaline pumping through me, preparing me for a fight, subsides. Emilia catches up to me, a smile across her face, watching the scene before us. She wraps her arms around my waist, attempting to stifle her giggles and silently laughs. Looking back at Milori's impromptu dance, I can't help but chuckle, too. By this point, Milori stops and turns to Garrick, who is trying to stand back up after laughing so hard on the ground.

"I repeat, what in the FAIRY RING was that?!" With his hands on his hips, he stares down at Garrick, who is smiling from ear to ear.

"A wake-up call. Didn't you say you didn't want to sleep in?"

"I SAID to gently wake me up in the morning because I'm not A MORNING PERSON! Not to throw a rodent into my tent!" Garrick starts to chuckle again.

"I mean, you never told us how to wake you up. Besides, I think that little guy enjoyed the rousing it gave you."

By this point, the entire Noble Guard is laughing, and Milori is obviously annoyed, but he regains his composure, dusting off invisible dust and addressing the lot.

"Well, if you're done, let's eat and pack up." Milori glares at Garrick and then turns, mumbling to himself.

The clean-up and breakfast take only a little bit of time, and then we're off flying again, heading towards Dorron. Cold air causes a shiver to run through my body, so I squeeze Emilia tighter to keep her warm. The sun's warm rays feel good on the skin, staving off the cold. We only fly for a few hours before a mountain peak comes into view. According to Milori, Dorron is on the other side, sitting between the valleys of the two mountains. Cresting over the mountain's peak, a valley comes into view. A large river runs between the two mountains, with round shelters peppering the area. Smoke rises from the chimneys of the houses, carrying the aroma of cooking meat towards us. It certainly smells better than the dried grains we eat this morning. The Southern Orcs live semi-nomadic lives, only travelling when the mines dry up. The main settlement of the Southern Orcs has been here for nearly one hundred years. Their housing can be easily disassembled, but some structures are permanent, always leaving a pattern of where they've settled and moved.

Orcs are coming out of their homes and taking us in from the ground. In the centre of town, there's a larger circular home with other structures attached to it. It's bigger than the other buildings, so I assume this is where the chief lives. My assumption proves correct when Milori leads us to the centre of the settlement, landing almost directly in front of the largest building. A large Orc man, likely seven feet tall and certainly taller than me, walks out bare-chested, with fur cloth and some cotton trousers wrapped around his waist. He's flanked by two equally large Orcs who are there to protect or counsel him. I'm unsure which, as Orc tradition and culture aren't something I know well. Garrick practically leaps out of Milori's arms. I suppose it might be embarrassing to be carried in by the Fae. Garrick moves his blade to his front while Emilia also pulls the blades under her tunic to her front. Looking around, the Noble Guard must pick up on the importance of the action because they, too, do as Garrick and Emilia do.

"Throm-ka." The chief steps towards our group, and though we agreed to meet and discuss the situation, I don't trust him. I step in front of Emilia and place myself in front of the group.

"Greetings. I'm sure there's no issue, but I would appreciate it if you would maintain a respectable distance from my spirit bond." The fact that we haven't completed the ceremony puts me on edge. The chief stops and assesses me, my men and my spirit bond, the latter causing me irritation. My markings start to glow slightly. Though I know it's not a problem and no one wishes us harm, the other part of my brain doesn't want to be rational.

"I am Ruk, the chief of the Southern Orcs. Thank you, Dorgan Garrick, for your respectful appearance." I side-eye Garrick, who steps up towards Ruk and stretches out his arm. Ruk grasps his forearm while Garrick does the same. Garrick clenches a fist and smacks it on his chest. Ruk grunts. This must be some sort of greeting. Emilia tries to step around me, but my instinct to protect her hasn't waned, and I hold her hand in mine. Ruk turns to Emilia, making me bristle at his attention to her, and he nods in her direction in greeting.

"Dorgan Emilia, throm-ka. As your bond is untrusting, I'll greet you from afar, but know you're welcome in my house. Come, we have food prepared. We'll discuss your father inside." We head into the building, but Emilia squeezes my arm. I look down at her to see a concerned face.

"What's the matter, my flower?"

"You should have let me greet him. He's still my chief." She worries the inside of her lip as she watches everyone head inside.

"My flower, they know how bonds work. He knows that it's challenging for me to see you close to another male."

"But it was fine with the Noble Guard." Sighing as quietly as I can, I try to think of a way to explain this to her.

"I'm sorry, my darling. I'm more jealous than I should be. My men are under my command, and I trust them. I don't trust this chief, and though I'm unsure of the customs of the Orc, one thing is certain between our races: we value and respect the bond between two people. Please forgive me for being a touch possessive. You've become everything to me, and I don't wish to kill someone because they came too close to you. I hope my agitation will dwindle after the bonding ceremony, but I'm not known to be someone who shares well, so I likely won't change." I give my most remorseful face, which is enough for Emilia to smile contentedly at me. She reaches up and pulls me down into a sweet kiss. Her lips are soft and make the agitation building inside of me subside. The amount of power this woman has over me is concerning, but I wouldn't change it at all.

"I'm yours, my scary Fae king." She winks at me and starts heading into the building, hand in mine, pulling me along. I think she just gives me a nickname. That makes me far too satisfied, even if it says I'm scary, but it also says I'm hers.

The floor is made of stone, and a fire pit sits in the middle, boiling soup that smells very appetizing. A large table sits on the far side of the room where Milori is seated, along with Garrick. Another table sits off to the side where the Noble Guard sit, assessing their surroundings like good soldiers. There are two empty seats beside Ruk and one beside that, which I assume are for Emilia and me. I lead her to the seats, pulling one out so she can sit down first and then take the seat next to her. Ruk looks over to the side and raises a finger. Light drumming begins, and a couple of Orc women pour out, bringing food to the table.

"I hope you don't mind. We like to serve food to our guests as soon as they've arrived." Plates of seared and marinated meat are placed on the table. Roasted root vegetables accompany them. The food looks hearty, like the Orc people, whereas the Fae tend to like lighter foods. Either way, the giant smile on Emilia's face tells me I may have to adjust our usual dinner menu, especially considering how happy she is to see this food.

"Roasted venison... fried rutabaga... these are my favourites," Emilia whispers under her breath, and her joy makes my heart joyous. I'm grateful to see her happy with how much she's endured this past year. The food is good, though a bit heavy in my stomach. After the meal, many of those who sit with us to eat leave, leaving a handful of Orcs and my guard behind. We move to a small room attached to the larger communal area with chairs and lounging furniture covered in furs and tightly woven blankets. I find a spot where Emilia and I can sit together. Ruk sits across from us with a drink in his hand.

"My scout gives me a report of your interest in Ezuren. To say I was surprised that the Day Court King was poking around is an understatement, but perhaps we can help each other. We have the same enemy, after all." He's a shrewd man, taking advantage of this situation, but what he doesn't seem to understand is that I can go in and get Dorgan Zornak out unassisted. It just may cost hundreds of lives. Now, I don't want to do that, but I would in order to save him. I haven't considered this seriously because it wouldn't make Emilia happy, and I'll try to avoid upsetting her if possible.

"I will not be coerced into joining a war between the Orcs. We have no reason to become involved. One of your spies informed me that you would be willing to give us information on guard rotations and the specific location of Emilia's father. Now, if your requirement for that information is to become involved in a war we have nothing to do with, then the answer is no. We'll go into Ezuren and find him ourselves. I don't know how much you know of me or my abilities, but I'm very capable of handling any situation that arises." Ruk assesses me, leaving a long pause hanging in the air.

"I don't wish to lose my honour over something like this. The goddess is already displeased with Dorgan Zornak, who has been captured and forced to work for Gormash." Ruk spits on the ground, saying the name of the other chief. "Dorgan Zornak is an honourable Orc who fought alongside me during many wars with the Northern Clan. I owe it to him to see his liberation. I ask for forgiveness from Dorgan Garrick and Dorgan Emilia for being unable to do anything sooner. By the time we knew what was going on, you were being watched too heavily, and Zornak had been imprisoned in Ezuren, a city we couldn't penetrate yet. My scouts will share the layout of the city and the guard rotations with you. I've arranged for you to meet one of my spies outside the city early tomorrow morning before dawn. He'll take you inside and show you the way."

"Thank you." Emilia has entwined our fingers at this point. I knew she was nervous when I refused to give in to the subtle request, but I wouldn't be backed into a corner.

"We Orcs aren't known for being politically knowledgeable, but within our customs, a conversation needs to be had if you hope to bond with a clansman. She may not be an Orc by blood, but she's one of us. I won't demand anything from you because I've heard of your powers, and frankly, I like my house, so I'll request that we meet and discuss an alliance. You may not want to get involved in the Orc wars, but I'm afraid the Orcs are already a part of the war you're fighting at home. We've gained more than just information on the humans trying to take over our lands; we also know of some of the inner workings of the Night Court."

He doesn't seem to be trying to antagonize me; he's merely stating what he knows. Though I hate to admit it, Emilia was raised by Orcs, so for that reason, I'll entertain this thought.

"After we rescue Zornak, you'll be invited to the Palace. We'll discuss a potential alliance then." Seemingly satisfied with that, he nods and stands, the rest of us following suit.

"We've made space for you to rest before your flight tonight. My understanding is you'll need to leave at the height of the night?"

"That's correct, and I would like to ask that Emilia stay here and be protected while we're away." Emilia's hand tightens around mine, stronger than I was expecting. I don't share this part of the plan with her, but I can't focus if she's there. I hope she'll understand that.

"Of course. She'll be safe here. My wife will make sure she's well tended to." We all leave with a nod of his head, and our group is escorted to another similar building with a series of small rooms off the main area. The men fan out to find a space to rest before our departure tonight. I escort Emilia to a small room with a twin bed and a window, which gives a lovely view of the mountains.

"I'm going with you." She releases my hand and walks to the other side of the room. I figure I would have to convince her to stay, but I don't like the amount of anger in her voice.

"My flower,"

"Don't you 'my flower' me. This is MY father! I want to be there!" Behind her anger, fear surfaces, which pulls me across the small space to wrap her in my arms.

"My flower, I know that staying here is the last thing you want to do, but let me ask you how you see your involvement in the rescue." My question isn't to belittle her but to help her see that staying here is better and safer.

"Well, I know how to sneak around. I've done that for the past year, haven't I? I also know how to use a weapon when need be." Her last response is weaker than the first.

"As great as those skills are, what would you do if we were in the middle of a fight?"

"...so, I don't know how to fight...but I don't want to be left behind. Besides, you'll make sure nothing happens to me." A surge of pride fills me, knowing she trusts me enough to protect her.

"You're right. I would protect you. In fact, I would protect you over your father." That makes her still, the words sinking in. "I can't focus on rescuing your father while I constantly check to make sure you're safe. I promise I'll bring him to you as fast as possible, my flower." A small tear escapes her eye. I wipe it away and kiss the track it left on her cheek. She leans her head onto my chest and takes a deep breath in.

"And you'll come back with him?" She whispers into my chest.

"I will, and Garrick too. I doubt Milori will let anything happen to any of us. When he goes into a fight, he's methodical and vicious." She looks up at me, surprised because, unless you've seen Milori fight, you would never expect the carnage he can cause. I don't want her last memory of us to be this, so I lean down and take her lips in mine. She gasps at the surprise affection which spurs me on. Wrapping my arms around her body, I pull her close, relishing the feel of my spirit bond in my arms. She melts into my embrace and, for a moment, the pressure of the circumstance melts away as well. But it's just that, a moment, and the strain of it all comes crashing back on us. Reluctantly pulling away, I take her face in my hands instead.

"I love you, Emilia. Even if I didn't have a strong bond with you, I've grown to love every aspect of you: your loyalty, perseverance, kindness, and even your snappy tongue. I love everything about you. I'm honoured to be able to bring your father back to you, which I will do. You'll be with your family again, Emilia. I promise." Her watery smile brings me peace, but I'm shocked by what she says next.

"I think I love you too, Timas. I don't know how much of this is the bond or just getting to know you and being able to trust you, but somewhere along the way, I think I started falling in love with you." Sweeping her up in my arms, I hug her tightly, burying my face in her hair. She loves me!

"You can never know how happy you've made me, Emilia." Still holding her off the ground, I kiss her again. When we part this time, I know it's for the necessity of rest, to be best prepared for what faces us tonight.

"Say goodbye before you go?" Brushing the hair out of her face, I can't help but touch her.

"I will." One last kiss, and I head to the room designated for me, which, surprisingly, is bigger than the one I left Emilia in. One day, I won't need to leave her. That day can't come soon enough.

Chapter 22

Timas

The moon sits high in the sky as we prepare to leave. Emilia comes out with something wrapped in her hands. I open my arms for her to walk into, and she does so gladly.

"What do you have there, my flower?" Popping her head up to look at me, with the item she carries scrunched between us, she says,

"It's a cloak for Father. It's a bit cold flying, and I wanted him to be warm." Her thoughtfulness, in turn, warms me.

"We'll take it with us." She ducks her head against my chest with a smile on her face.

"Thank you."

With everything sorted and a plan to meet our contact outside the city, I kiss Emilia one last time and set off for Ezuren. Garrick grumbles as Milori directs him to one of the Noble Guards to be carried by. The two of them act like they've known each other for years, although they're newly acquainted. However, Milori is good at breaking down people's barriers and forcing himself in.

The night is extremely dark. There are no stars in the sky to add any light, and clouds partially cover the moon. The entire flight, I think about what's to come. Ideally, we'll be able to go in quietly and leave quietly. I have no desire to destroy a city. From what the scout said, there's an unguarded entrance into the city through the water system. A wall surrounds the city, and only two main entrances allow access to the city, which are both heavily guarded. Though I would prefer not to wade through the water, it's far more ideal than trying to go unnoticed at the gates or trying to avoid the watchmen who walk the ramparts.

In the distance, I can see lights that spread across the dark sky: our destination is in sight. We'll meet the Southern Orc contact outside the city in an apple orchard. The group flies in a staggered pattern with five guards, Milori, myself, and Garrick, still being carried begrudgingly. Milori takes a sharp turn and descends into a dark, clouded area. The closer we get, the more branches start to materialize. The quiet sound of eight sets of feet land in the middle of the orchard. Milori hand signals to have the men fan out. The area is silent, and there's no light nearby to brighten the space, but the just-visible moon provides a dim outline of the trees. A cool breeze flows through the trees, and a large figure enters the clearing. He's far quieter than I was expecting. Orcs aren't known for their agility or ability to nimbly go from place to place like the Fae, so my surprise at his appearance isn't unwarranted.

"King Timas?" The deep voice and the large figure immediately tell me he's an Orc, and the only reasonable assumption is that this is our contact.

"Yes. You're to help us get inside?" He walks closer to me, his appearance becoming clearer. He's wearing a heavy leather apron and a fairly torn-up shirt. It's a common theme to have Orc spies as the blacksmith. I remember that I need to have the blacksmith in Sonas investigated after this.

"We don't have long. The guard rotation will change just before dawn. The ones on duty now are tired and will more than likely be sleeping." He's gruff and to the point, which would aggravate me in another situation, but right now, I want to get this over with so I can get back to Emilia. The itching under my skin is starting to irritate me, and an anxious feeling in my stomach flares the moment we take off. If I didn't know any better, I would think the bond between Emilia and me is already complete, but I can't see how that would be possible without the ceremony. Without the tying of our souls eternally together, there should be no way I can feel Emilia. Rolling my shoulders and slightly shaking my head, I try to refocus on the task at hand. The Orc, who doesn't introduce himself or give his name, turns around and starts heading into the night. Apparently, he isn't one of the chatty Orcs. I look over at Milori, and his response is a simple shrug as he follows behind the Orc. Garrick, on the other hand, has more to say than my second-in-command. I may need to rethink the command structure for the future.

"Oi, Kin. Listen, I understand you haven't had a lot of trust-worthy interactions lately, but you're leading the King of the Day Court into the heart of Ezuren. An explanation of what we'll see and what to expect should be, at a minimum, what you should be doing right now. If time is of the essence, speak quickly." Garrick's tone is clipped and has a slight edge to it. Perhaps just following along would have been better than challenging the man who's supposed to show us a shortcut into the city. My concerns are immediately assuaged when the unnamed Orc turns around, crosses his arms over his chest, and gives a quick nod. I'll need to study Orc customs because that's obviously not how I would have dealt with the situation.

"Gormash has kept a suffocating collar on the people of Ezuren for the past few months. As the invasion draws nearer, it becomes increasingly difficult to freely navigate the city. The guard rotations have been sporadic and, at times, hard to track, but after some time, we've been able to pick up a pattern of sorts. As for the location of Dorgan Zornak, he's being held in the inner city, which is also surrounded by a thick stone wall. This won't be a simple task to get in and back out again. The inner city is for those closest to Gormash. It has its own private taverns and blacksmith, which is currently being run by Dorgan Zornak. He's not in good health, as far as we can tell. They restrict his diet to enough to keep him alive and working and they're working him hard. He's unnaturally thin for an Orc, but he pushes through, no doubt, to keep his daughter alive. If he resists or acts up in any way, they beat him. If that doesn't work, they threaten a daughter he has, saying they'll kill her if he doesn't keep working or being quiet, in some cases. We were able to get a message to him, telling him to expect company tonight. If that's enough explanation, let us go and help him." With another tight nod, he turns and heads back into the darkness. Garrick trails behind, his shoulders tense. A wave of heat flows through me, thinking about the Orcs who threatened my Emilia. I hope they're the ones guarding him tonight.

The unnamed Orc leads us to a grated hole in the city's wall. It seems a bit small for an oversized Orc to fit through, but he surprises me, not for the first time tonight, by pulling the grate off and crawling into the hole. Each of us follows behind him, crawling on our hands and knees until we reach an area in which we can't quite stand, but can at least crouch. We aren't in the tunnel long before we hit a wall with a ladder going to the street. Quietly, we follow until we're all on the street level behind a dilapidated home. From the window, moderately lit up by a light inside, another Orc looks out. He must be able to see us because he nods to the Orc leading us. Something passes between them before we set off down a narrow alleyway behind a row of buildings just as run-down as the house we came up behind. The Noble Guard vigilantly looks at and assesses every street light, alleyway, and drunken patron roaming the streets. The Guard flanks me while Milori and Garrick walk ahead. Fifteen minutes of weaving between buildings and hiding in the shadows finally leads us to another wall within the city. Just like the Orc said, it's a city inside of a city with its own thick wall and a single gate going in and out. My heart beats a little bit faster, anticipating the fight ahead of us, but taking deep breaths and focusing on the immediate task of getting into this section of the city takes precedence.

The Orc walks right up to the main gate. Confused, I scan our surroundings to check for any potential threats or if the Orc is leading us into a trap. The Noble Guard senses the change and also takes in our surroundings. A quick whistle goes out into the night, sparking the power within me. If this Orc has set us up, he'll be the first one I kill. A quick whistle is returned, and the side door beside the gate opens. The nameless Orc gestures towards the door, indicating to proceed. He enters first, and although I'm still waiting for a trap, crossing over seems as quiet as before. The inner city is less crowded, with fewer buildings. There's a guardhouse and a courtyard with a stage and sharp tools. Glancing at the gruesome display, I decide I don't want to guess what the tools are for. The main building, which looks more like a fortified castle, looms in front of us and just off to the right sits a building with a forge in front. Orcy, because calling him an unnamed Orc is starting to bother me, leads us in the shadows behind a handful of buildings to the right. We come to the edge of a building and see an open space between where we are and where the blacksmith is.

A guard lazily sits on a chair beside the door, foot crossed over his knee as he nods off. Milori steps in front of Orcy and decidedly takes over this portion of the rescue. Milori motions for two of the Guard to circle around the back of the building and sends one to the side of the blacksmith facing us. The one in front walks, with no sound, to the Orc sitting guard. A soft white glow comes from his hand, and, reaching toward his chest, he pulls. The Orc guard quickly wakes up and clutches his throat, but before too much noise is made, the Fae Guard has twisted and snapped his neck. He can manipulate air and can take the air from one's lungs. It isn't the best way to die, but breaking his neck makes sure he doesn't suffer long. Quietly righting him in the chair, he looks over his shoulder, and Milori leads the rest of us across the open space.

Orcy trails behind us with Garrick. The look on his face shows his shock at the efficiency of my Guard. This is nothing compared to what they're fully capable of, but he doesn't need to know that. The front door to the blacksmith is opened as we file in. Light comes from a small room to the right and a door to the left. Orcy motions to the door, which likely leads down to the basement where Zornak is being held. I look at Milori and indicate I'm heading that way. With a nod of acknowledgement, I quietly walk to the door. It creaks slightly, but the muted thumping noise behind me likely means Milori takes care of whatever (or whomever) is in the room. I descend a dark set of stairs with Garrick following me. The stairs turn at a corner, and another door sits before me. My power thrums underneath my skin, causing my markings to glow slightly. Zornak is likely behind this door, but so is another guard or two. Whatever happens, I need to act quickly and decisively. Opening the door, a single light sits on a table in the corner, and just as I suspected, a guard sits there. He's nearly asleep, but the noise of opening the door brings him to attention. His eyes widen in shock and he grabs at his sword. Power deep inside me roars to life. Trying to control how much the ground shakes, I shoot out my hand, sending electricity through the Orc's body. He convulses from the shock, giving me time to get closer to ending his life. Before I make it to him, a sharp pain pierces my side, and though I can barely feel pain in this heightened state, I notice it. I was too preoccupied with the one enemy that I didn't take in the rest of the room to see another Orc coming out of the shadows, striking me in the side. Garrick jumps in and grabs him from behind, wrestling him, but ends up twisted around and is in a headlock in front of the guard. I reach out and throw the offending Orc at the wall, giving Garrick enough time to send his fist into his torso and begin eviscerating his face.

Turning back to the initial Orc I had attacked, I find him on the ground, shaking but trying to push himself up off the floor. Before he makes it up, I deliver a swift kick and send him into the wall, giving me plenty of time to pull out my dagger and drive it into his heart. Ripples of lightning jump off my skin. I need to be careful. If I let too much power out, then I'll call a storm of great magnitude to this location, burning everything in sight. Breathing heavily, I look around the room again and find a man sitting on a thin mat, chained by his feet to the wall behind him. By now, Garrick has finished off the other guard and races over to the sickly man.

"Father!" Garrick lands on his knees before his father; his voice hitched with restrained emotion. The man, Zornak, reaches out and wraps his arms around Garrick. I was under the impression that they aren't a physically affectionate race, but apparently, I'm misinformed.

"Garrick, my son. Are you alright?" He pushes him back, inspecting his face and body, taking in every cut, scratch and bruise he sustained from attacking the other guard.

"I'm fine, Father, but you aren't." A pang of jealousy shoots through me. Though I had a good father, he never looked at me with such care as Zornak looks at his son. How much more so will he be glad to see my Emilia? Garrick's observation is correct. His thin and frail body has sustained many injuries. It's a wonder he's able to sit up properly.

"The key. We need to find the key." Before Garrick can get up to rummage through this dark and dirty basement, I walk over and place my hand on the metal around his ankles. The magnitude of strength I pull from the earth courses through my arm and down my hand, snapping the metal easily. Zornak looks up at me then with a curious eye.

"A Fae man here to rescue an insignificant Orc. How the days have changed."

"You aren't insignificant to my spirit bond. If you're important to her, you're important to me." His eyes widen in shock, appraising me again, likely assessing my worthiness for his daughter. He turns to look at Garrick, who's pulling the chains out from around his father.

"This is King Timas of the Day Court and Emilia's spirit bond." His eyes swing back to me.

"Well, I didn't see that coming." Weakly, he pushes up, trying to stand.

"Yes, many have been surprised, but surprise or not, she's the other half of my spirit and she wants her father, so I'm going to take you to her. I don't know how much longer we have. Are you able to walk?" Garrick supports his father, but he stands and looks stronger. This man is made of more robust metal than white iron.

"I'll manage. Let's go. It's been too long since I saw my daughter."

Retracing our steps, we head back up to the main floor, where the Noble Guard is waiting for us when we reach the top of the stairs. Once Garrick and Zornak make it up from the basement, Milori looks around and makes a plan.

"The Orc that led us here has returned to wherever he came from. He doesn't wish to be found out if possible. The gate is open and should be easy enough to get through, and then we'll retrace our steps back to the water system that led us inside." Slightly annoyed that Orcy didn't stick around, I take in the sky. It has lightened significantly since arriving.

"Did Orcy tell you when the guard change was? If anyone comes here, they're going to see a lot of dead Orcs."

"Orcy?" Milori looks at me in confusion, and I wave him off.

"He never told us his name. I had to come up with something."

"How original." He snorts.

"Can we go if you two are done debating the man's pet name?" Garrick says. Milori takes in Zornak and quickly changes his demeanour. Leading us back out the front door, we manage to get behind the buildings that will take us to the gate. But before we can reach the door, an alarm sounds, and a roar comes from the blacksmith building.

"They figured out their guys are dead," Milori says.

"That's it. No more sneaking around. We're leaving," I say, moving to the front and heading towards the gate. As the gate comes into sight, several Orcs pour through it, and I'm beyond angry at this point. The restraint I've put on my power has pulled tightly at my skin, either that or my body craves to be near my spirit bond. It's nearly impossible to discern which at this moment. My markings glow even brighter, and the ground shakes beneath my feet. The Noble Guard can accommodate the sudden change, but the Orcs cannot. Most fall to the ground and some scramble to stay on their feet but fail. Lightning courses through me, the arc of power jumping off my skin. One Orc locks eyes with me, and pure terror crosses his face. Pulling as much energy as possible, I slam it into the group of Orcs, still trying to maintain their balance. A bright light explodes from the impact, and part of the wall crumbles to rubble behind them. I don't even look back, knowing the Noble Guard will follow behind me, bringing Zornak and Garrick along with them. When the power that lies inside finally finds its release, it's hard to rein it back in, but I don't want to rein it in. I want to destroy the people who've hurt my Emilia and her family this past year. Milori yells at everyone to follow him, but I'm not paying attention.

A large Orc comes running out of the castle, roaring at people to attack. The scar that brands his face and the fierce look on his face means only one thing: this must be Gormash. A wave of unbridled rage courses through me, sending a shockwave across the courtyard. I topple the barracks beside the sorry excuse for a castle, causing significant damage to its structure. The pieces fly and take Gormash to the ground. A feeling of justice builds in me, but I want to make sure he's dead. I would prefer to make his death long and painful. Turning my feet in Gormash's direction, I'm stopped in my tracks by the call of Milori.

"Timas! Come on! Emilia wants you back!" The mere mention of her name makes me halt in my pursuit of the man who's been tormenting my beautiful flower. I promised her I would bring her father home, and I promised I would come back too. Turning on my heels, I walk quickly to Milori, still standing near Garrick and Zornak.

"No sense waiting until we're outside the walls. We need to fly out now." Two Noble guards gather around Garrick and Zornak, and we lift up into the cold morning air. The flight back will be challenging, but we've trained well and will make it back. Just as we get above the city, another roar of anger rings out in the air. Gormash hasn't been killed, which tempts me into a return flight. Arrows are whistling through the air now as ground forces use crossbows to try and drop us from the sky.

They're easy enough to miss, but one arrow grazes Milori's side. He yells in pain and begins to lose elevation. Manoeuvring over to him, I get close enough to see him struggling to maintain his path. His side is leaking blood, and he's starting to look pale, a sure sign that the injury was caused by a white iron arrow. Out of anger, I let out a massive cry, which shakes the ground beneath us. In one swift move, I pull Milori from the air and carry him in my arms. He doesn't fight me, which tells me how bad it must be, but he's conscious enough to make a joke.

"At least take me out for dinner before we cuddle." His words are strained, but I pull a tight smile because he needs it, and I need to get him help quickly.

"You're too high maintenance." He scoffs at that.

"At least this will mean lots of ladies will want to come see the hero of the Day Court! Let's not tell them it was a stray arrow that got me. Let's say I jumped in front of you to protect you. That sounds far more heroic."

I shake my head at what is clearly a coping mechanism.

"You are a hero, Milori. No one could put up with me like you do." A tightness pulls in my chest. He's been there for me for centuries, and I won't let one single arrow be why I lose him.

"Stop it! Don't go all mushy on me. That's supposed to be the job of the many ladies who will fawn over me. Now, get me home, horsey. I want a bath." Glad to see he hasn't lost his sense of humour, I fly hard toward Dorron.

Chapter 23

Emilia

I have been pacing the floor since before dawn. In the early morning, I was startled awake, and a spike of adrenaline coursed through me. I didn't know why, but I couldn't fall asleep after that. I feel anxious knowing that whatever is happening, there's a chance something could go terribly wrong. What if they get there and can't find my father, or what if something happens to Timas? The fear twists in my stomach like someone has reached in and placed my insides in a vice. These walls seem to be closing in on me, and I decide that a walk may be my only hope for distraction. Stepping out into the morning, the smell of spring fills my senses as the chilly air hits my face. The shock of the cool air hitting my lungs removes a bit of the panic that has been slowly growing inside me.

A small sitting area to my right has a table, chairs, and fur hanging over a wooden fence nearby. A cough startles me out of my thoughts. Looking up, I see an Orc woman standing before me. She has ornate beads braided into her hair, a large nose ring, and dark black paint around her eyes: this is the chief's wife.

"Throm-ka, Dorgan Emilia."

"Throm-ka, Lady Chief." She sets a tray of food and a mug full of hot liquid on the small table.

"No need to be so formal, Emilia. You're a clansman. My name is Borgha. You must be hungry, so eat." Her gruff tone is typical of an Orc woman, so I'm not offended when she commands me to eat. The food smells good, especially the freshly baked bread, so I take a chunk, break off a small piece, and place it in my mouth. The bread has a strong yeast taste. It's a nostalgic sensation, but it only reminds me of my father and sours my mood further.

"You won't make them return quicker by pacing the ground." She sits at the table and grabs the other mug of likely warm malt beer. Reluctantly, I sit as well and grab the second mug. The warm, slightly sweet taste coats my mouth. I didn't realize how thirsty I was. Along with discovering my own thirst, a growl from my stomach makes itself known. Grabbing a piece of cheese, I put it onto the bread I already served myself and, very impolitely, shove the whole portion into my mouth.

"You're quite famous." I stop momentarily chewing my food and look over at Borgha. I don't know what she's saying. Maybe I've become well known since discovering I'm the spirit bond to the King of the Day Court?

"I didn't really choose to become Timas' spirit bond." She lightly shakes her head and takes another sip.

"No, you were well-known far before you met him. Your story is told across the clans. The story of Dorgan Zornak is an example of why Orcs shouldn't get involved with humans. Though his standing and respect as a warrior could never be diminished, he changed after the pain of his youth." My brow scrunches together as I take in her words. Is she saying my father having a human daughter should be something to be ashamed of? I knew he was treated differently because of me and that some, well, many, people commented on the odd choice of raising a human, but I hadn't heard that his life was an example of 'what not to do.'

"Don't take some great offence. This was before you, when your father met your mother. Sylvia was her name, correct?"

"What do you mean?" Father never really talks about the time he spent with my mother. All he's ever said is that he once thought they would be together forever, but that isn't what happened.

"Your father was a high-ranking warrior in the Clan at one time. One of his scouting trips led him to the river that bordered the human kingdom. The story goes that he stumbled upon a young human woman curled up by the river bank, wearing rags for clothes and looking sickly. Despite Dorgan Zornak's reputation as a cold and brutal warrior, he saw something in this frail woman and brought her back to his home. He tended to her, fed and clothed her, and they fell in love. Many had scoffed at the idea that he would take a chosen bond, but he was undeterred in his affection for your mother. Years passed, and no binding ceremony took place, but she stayed and eventually became pregnant with Dorgan Garrick. They had quite the family for a while, but she was never really accepted into our

Clan. Many didn't believe it was a good idea to inter-bond with the humans and instead used that prejudice to make her life difficult. I believe Dorgan Garrick was three when she disappeared into the night. Zornak mourned her for years and became a shell of a man. The fierce warrior he once was disappeared the very same night she did. He went from being a warrior to becoming a blacksmith, a very good one, but his drive to fight left with her that night. Then, to everyone's surprise, she returned with a daughter all those years later." My head is swimming, making me feel dizzy. I've had little sympathy for my mother since she left me all those years ago, but what she would have gone through must have been so difficult. The fear of not being accepted by the Fae rises to my mind as she continues the story.

"It was quite an event to see her return with a small child. Some speculated that you were Zornak's somehow and were cursed to look like a human, but that was quickly put to an end by the elders. This time, she didn't stick around a full day and left in the night, leaving you behind. But you know that part. You might not know that you gave him a new purpose and life. He took to you quickly, even fought many who said he should get rid of you and that you weren't his responsibility. He stood strong and immediately claimed you as his daughter, even going to the temple to make it official just days after meeting you. After your family moved to the Mogd, on the border, the story took on a life of its own. Dorgan Zornak was no longer ridiculed for falling in love with a human, but he was respected for raising Garrick and a weak human to be good Orcs. Though the story still stands as a way to discourage the young from seeking a bond with a human, it also represents loyalty, faithfulness and strength."

I hadn't realized I was crying until a tear falls on my hand. Being called weak isn't unusual compared to the Orc people. I am, but it hits me differently when thinking about what Father did for me. He's been a shield for our family for so many years, and he was just left to rot in Ezuren. Chief Ruk should have done something, a thought that greatly angers me. I won't feel better until I know for sure that my father is safe and away from the Northern Orcs.

"My father is a great man. The story that circulates is just that: a story. I'm glad many people respect him, but he's more than just a warrior or a great blacksmith to me. He's an example of someone taking in an orphan he didn't have to and loving her. He's always been my protector, and he taught me to stand up for those you love, no matter what."

"A good lesson to learn. I'm afraid you'll need that unmoving love in the future."

"What's that supposed to mean?"

"It means the King of the Day Court has a war coming, and he'll need someone to stand beside him while he faces the onslaught of attacks. I suspect your loyalty to each other will be tested. It's good that he'll be bonded to a woman raised by an Orc who values such loyalty. Only an Orc can do it well. You'll need to be steadfast for the challenges ahead of you."

Is this about the problem going on in Sonas? Timas hasn't really mentioned what's happening. I was so consumed by what was happening in my life that I never even asked what was happening in his. Guilt sinks deep in my stomach; for someone who's the other half of a person's spirit, I haven't been considering his own pressures. I resolve even in that moment to support Timas as he's supported me. Before we can continue the conversation, the drums ring loudly from the towers. Quickly, I stand and run further into the settlement, my eyes on the sky, searching for my father and the man I've fallen in love with. Mere specks in the sky show larger than normal birds, but they're coming in quickly, and their shape grows to show the Noble Guard and three people being carried. That can't be right. Only Father and Garrick can't fly. My hands shake slightly. The only reason I can think of for another person to be carried is if they're injured. An image of Timas pops into my mind, bruised and wounded. The group descends and lands softly, as I'm sure they've practiced a hundred times. The first guard I notice sets a thin-looking man down on his feet. The man stands upright, his brown eyes turn in my direction, and my entire world just about spins out of control. My legs take off in a run. Father! He opens his arms to me, his smile and watery eyes hitting me right in the heart. I finally reach him, wrapping my arms around his body and sob uncontrollably into his chest as he lowers us to the ground. Wrapped up in the protection of my father's arms, I feel relief now, having my family safe and whole.

Pulling back, I take in his sunken cheeks and the bruises that litter his body, all in different stages of healing.

"Father! You're hurt!" I barely choke out.

"I'm fine, little swallow, but he isn't." Looking up, I see Timas holding a limp Milori. Scrambling to my feet, I race over to them.

"What happened?" I notice blood coming from Milori's side. A chill passes through my body looking at his wound.

"They shot white iron arrows at us as we left. Milori was grazed by one. The cut isn't deep, but it looks like the arrows were dipped in a liquid form of white iron, which has spread and is infecting the area." An Orc herbalist pushes her way through the crowd of onlookers.

"Move ye big ole oafs, let me see h'm." A large Orc woman with a satchel in her hands approaches us. I step out of the way so she can look at Milori. Milori starts to move a bit, tipping his head in the direction of the herbalist.

"This wasn't the wake-up call I was hoping for. Where are all the pretty ladies?" My mouth drops open at the blatant insult he gives the old herbalist, but she laughs as she pulls at the fabric around the wound.

"Afraid ya get me. I may be old, but I's got some spring still left in me yet." She waves for someone to take Milori. Though reluctantly, Timas releases Milori into her care. I can't wait any longer. I fling myself into Timas' arms, embracing him fiercely. I want him to feel the happiness and relief he's given me by bringing my father back and returning safely himself. He lifts my head and cradles my face in his hands. He takes my mouth in a searing kiss, his tongue exploring my mouth, testing its depths and showing me how much I mean to him. Unspoken messages of fear and relief, of trial and victory, of need and want, pass between us. Breathlessly pulling away, he pulls me closer to hold me tight again.

"Thank you. Thank you so much, Timas." I can't seem to get the wobble out of my voice, but he doesn't care.

"Anything for you, my flower, anything." He kisses the top of my head, causing warmth to spread across my body.

"Will Milori be okay?"

"I believe so. So long as the herbalist can clean the wound and give him the right herbal concoction, he'll be fine. I saw one of the guards go with him with supplies from the palace. We'll need to tell him, however, that he insulted the woman trying to help him." Smacking his chest, I look straight into his eyes.

"We will not! We'll be nice to him and make sure he has everything he needs. He was injured rescuing my father, after all."

"You're only going to contribute to his already annoying and whiny personality, you know. He doesn't need any encouragement."

"I agree with the King." Garrick's deep voice forces us to turn around. Garrick and Father stand side by side. Stretching out my arms, I wrap the only family I've ever had in them.

"I'm so glad you're both safe." I don't know how to explain my relief at seeing them standing in front of me. The weight that seemed permanently affixed to my shoulders has fallen off, knowing we won't be used against each other again.

"I'll go check on the pest and make sure he isn't insulting the entire camp with his big mouth." Garrick walks toward the herbalist's hut, leaving Father and Timas with me.

"King Timas, I don't think I can express in words how much it means to me that you've kept my children safe. You didn't need to risk your life and that of your men to rescue me, but I appreciate it nonetheless." Father sticks his hand out toward Timas. I suck in a breath because I didn't exactly explain Orc customs to him. Add that to the things I should have told him earlier, but Timas grabs Father's arm, Father reciprocates and shakes once. It's a form of respect shown between clan members for those you trust and acknowledge as a respectful Orc. Father hugs me tightly and walks away, showing his approval of Timas and trust in his ability to watch out for me. Timas turns his gaze to me.

"So, I guess he approves?" I laugh at his observation.

"Yes, he approves. How did you learn how to do that?"

"I saw your brother do it to the chief and figured that was the custom."

"Huh. You're a quick study." I mull that over for a moment.

"On some things, perhaps, but I'm afraid you're going to have to teach me more about the Orc customs, especially if I'm to continue having meetings with the chief later." I hum in agreement. "Now I need to find a bed. It's been a long night." We head toward the sleeping accommodations together. Taking a nap sounds wonderful, but seeing my father sounds better. So, as Timas goes off to sleep, I spend some much-needed time with my reunited family.

Chapter 24

Timas

We've spent the last few days in Dorron recovering from the eventful trip to Ezuren. Milori has healed well and is back to his chipper self. Emilia has been smiling nonstop for the past few days, and knowing I helped put it there makes me feel incredibly content. Today, we're heading back to Sonas, as I've received several messages from the council stating they're unhappy I left without informing them. The need for advisors is important to keep a balanced and people-centred monarch, but I know that had I informed them, they might have tried to stop me. It wasn't a risk I was willing to take. I understand that we need to focus on the murders, but I needed to do this for Emilia and for us.

Emilia, Zornak, and Garrick walk over, each wearing a smile. Emilia's eyes immediately meet mine, and her smile grows even larger.

"You ready, my flower?" She walks up beside me and holds my hand tightly.

"Mhmm." Looking over at Zornak, I see his (much healthier) face. Even in a short time, his colour has returned, and he looks much stronger.

"Like I said before, you're both invited to come and live at the palace with us. It may take some adjusting, but I'm sure it would mean a lot to Emilia to have you both there."

"We've spoken about your invitation and have decided that we'll join you, but on one condition." I didn't expect a condition to my offer, but the smile on Emilia's face leads me to believe it can't be that bad. Zornak looks over at Garrick before he continues.

"We'll move there if we can work as blacksmiths in your palace." A job? He wants a job?

"That's unnecessary. You're Emilia's family and will be taken care of accordingly."

"This is non-negotiable. Orcs aren't known for being sedentary beings. We'll work for you and you alone. We would also prefer to live outside the palace. I don't wish to feel constrained to one place again." His request is reasonable. It would seem foolish to say no.

"Agreed."

"Good. We'll set off for Sonas tomorrow and be there within a week before this celebration of your betrothal."

Emilia gives each of them a hug before returning to my side. At that point, Milori walks over, a grin on his face, looking to cause trouble as his attention falls to Emilia.

"Well, gorgeous lady, are you ready for another flight?" A growl rips from my throat as I stare down at my best friend. He's just standing there with an infuriating smile that needs punching, but seeing as he was recently hurt and freshly recovered, I try to restrain myself.

"I love how easy it is to rile you up. This is going to be fun." He turns and walks away while Emilia pulls my head down to meet hers in a sweet kiss. Instantly, I'm calm.

"Well, I guess that's a solid indication that she's your spirit bond." I raise my eyebrow questioningly at Zornak. Of course she is.

"You went all glowy again. Last time I saw that, you blew up a barrack." His comment makes me feel slightly embarrassed. I don't want Emilia to think I can't control my anger, though admittedly, sometimes I can't. She leans up and whispers into my ear.

"I find that strangely attractive... maybe you can show me how you do that?" Now, my embarrassment has turned into something else for this woman. She truly is my other half. After saying goodbye to Emilia's family and gathering with the Noble Guard, the chief walks over to send us off. Ruk and his wife stand side by side with a mask of indifference, although later, Emilia assures me they're happy. Orcs are strange.

"You're welcome to visit the Southern Orcs at any time. Thank you for causing so much trouble in Ezuren. Their invasion plans have been postponed. It seems that after your little display of power, the humans are wondering what problem the Fae have with the Northern Orc Clan. I suspect once the humans discover you were merely motivated to save your spirit-bond's father, they'll once again join forces and try to invade our lands. At least that's my thought. Either way, you've given us more time, and we'll look for other ways to undermine and prevent their attempts."

I can't help but smile a little at Gormash's issues. He deserves far more than that for what he did to Emilia. Perhaps one day, I can repay him for his actions properly.

"We'll be busy for a little while, but after our betrothal ceremony, please come to the palace. I would like to talk to you about what you know of the Night Court and see if there's anything we can do to help each other."

With a plan to meet again, we return to Sonas, the Day Court capital, our home.

We arrive back early the following morning. Thankfully, we're able to make the entire flight to the coast because I'm the only one with a passenger. Emilia sleeps in my arms during the flight and the boat ride back to the city. After returning to our beds and sleeping most of the day away, I awake to a package I had arranged for before we left for the mountains.

After much convincing, I finally motivate Emilia to go for a walk with me. We end up on the same balcony we were on for the lantern ceremony. It feels like it was just yesterday that we were curled up under the stars as the lanterns took the wishes of my people into the sky. The sun is setting, providing the perfect backdrop for what I'm about to do.

"I didn't realize how breathtaking the view was last time. Mind you, I was so nervous, I don't know if I could have paid any attention to all of this. It's beautiful." Pink, purple, and orange colours surround the sun as it sets the continent in a picturesque view. Somehow, the colour of the sky makes it seem like a better place than I know it is.

Walking up to the stone wall, I lean beside Emilia, facing away from the sun and looking down at the woman who brings more than enough light to my life.

"You're beautiful." Her cheeks go pink, so I drag a knuckle across one, enjoying the way she gets flustered by the compliment.

"Thank you." She says with a smile.

"I have something for you." Reaching into my robe, I pull out a small cloth bag. Pulling on the drawstrings, I open the mouth of the bag and pull out the ring I had ordered for her. A gold ring decorated in an intricate pattern full of yellow sapphires. She gasps when she sees it.

"I've been told that humans typically give their betrothed a ring as a symbol of their engagement, while Orcs exchange armbands. The Fae don't give such things because when we bond with someone, the magic that binds us creates markings on our hands, similar to the markings that decorate my body. That will happen to you, regardless."

"Will it hurt?" With a small smile, I shake my head.

"No, it won't hurt. You'll have an overwhelming feeling of connection when we complete the ceremony, and then you'll feel me inside you, or rather, you'll feel parts of my feelings, but that's for another day. I wanted to give you something that would show you that I meant what I said. I want to bond with you, cherish you, grow old with you, laugh with you, cry with you. Actually, I don't enjoy seeing you cry, so maybe not that." She chuckles as I continue, "These past couple of weeks have been chaotic and life-changing, but I wouldn't want to go back to the way it was before. For hundreds of years, I wondered where my spirit bond was, what she would be like and even if she would return my affections. As it was, you hadn't yet been born. You're beyond any beauty I've ever seen and, for the most part, do seem to be fond of me."

"I'm incredibly fond of you."

"That's comforting to hear from the woman I love. Not just the bond, but truly, the woman you are. The woman who will gladly become a spy to keep her father alive. The woman who patiently waited on a spoiled noble, which is likely a good thing because I suspect I can be incredibly demanding, the woman who smiles when she sees a garden full of flowers. I love you, my beautiful Emilia. Will you become my bonded and Queen to serve alongside me in this city you've found yourself in?"

Her eyes are glassy, causing my nerves to spike. I can't force her to bond with me, but I want her to, not because she wants to protect someone else, but because she loves me.

"Timas, I didn't expect to find something so wonderful when I came to Sonas. My mind and heart have been weighed down with the responsibility of keeping my father alive, but you took my problems as your own and solved them for me. I don't know how I'll ever be able to thank you. You put your own problems on hold for me. Though I questioned the wisdom of the choice, I saw in it the passion you had for me to put your words of affection into action. I don't know if my becoming Queen is truly a good idea or if I'll be accepted by the Fae, but it doesn't matter anymore. I want to be with you, and if I have to learn how to be a Fae Queen, I'll do it because you're worth it. I love you, and I'll happily become your bonded." No one has ever said that I'm worth it before. Everyone expects me to do it all, to be what they need, never really caring about who I am, but she does. I gently grab her hand and slide the ring onto her finger. I can't wait to see the markings on her hand after the ceremony, but until then, this will shout to everyone: Emilia is my betrothed. My lips find hers and press softly at first, but the growing passion for her surfaces as our kiss becomes more than celebratory. Our mouths dance together in a celebration of the promises we've made, even here on this balcony, and the anticipation of what is to come. The desire I have for her increases with each passing day and the bonding ceremony can't arrive soon enough. The sun sets on us, and all I can think to do is thank the sun for the treasure I hold in my arms.

Chapter 25

Emilia

It's been just over a week since we returned. A whirlwind of meetings and greeting new nobles has occupied our time, and I don't know how Timas does it all. He's always good at ensuring we have a moment together, even if it means sneaking off to the garden in between meetings. The council is split on how they feel about having a human Queen. Raza'l is very unhappy about it, but Timas ends the conversation before he rants too long. On a darker side, there has been another murder since we've returned. Timas is on edge, desperately wanting to protect his people but unable to. I can't imagine how helpless he must feel. He thinks the wedding will give his people, or rather, our people, something to celebrate. I hope he's right and this doesn't cause them any more concern.

But tonight, tonight is the celebration of our betrothal, and saying I'm nervous is an understatement. The doubts that live permanently in my mind have been playing nasty little tricks on me all day, and crawling back into bed and hiding under the covers sounds like a great idea. But I won't do it. I won't do it because I love Timas, and we'll face all the opposition together. Even a fancy, overwhelming party.

"I'm glad you chose the ivory dress. It looks so good with your beautiful brown hair." Sigrid brings in the dress I plan to wear tonight, a long, flowy dress with a heart-shaped neckline and long, wispy fabric that falls off the arms. Timas wasn't exaggerating when he said he wanted to spoil me with clothes and jewellery. I still don't love having so much, especially when others are without, but I've been able to rein him in on his spending. I never thought I would have to say that.

"I like it too, the fabric is so soft!" Sigrid unlaces the back, helping me step into the dress. I'm so grateful to have her with me. Timas ensured she had her own room right next to mine. I insisted she had somewhere nice to sleep and rest if she wanted. For too many years, she lived in a cramped room. I didn't want that to be her life anymore. She seems happy even though she's still waiting on a noble. I really don't have to guess. She told me she's happy. Sigrid doesn't like to sit around, so the fact that she gets to do something to keep herself busy makes her happy. I try to do my part by asking very little of her. I fidget with the side of my nail as she finishes lacing up the back. She catches me and lightly tugs at my fingers.

"You're going to do amazing. There's nothing to worry about." Easy for her to say! She doesn't have to stand up in front of hundreds of people tonight AND meet her future mother-in-law, who used to be Queen.

"Of course, because standing in front of hundreds of Fae people is so simple. Oh, and meeting the Queen Dowager is absolutely not worth worrying about." Huffing a breath, I occupy my hands with the stray fabric billowing around my arms.

"She's going to love you!" Sylphina walks in carrying pretty ivory shoes that will match the dress, but they're way too tall. I wonder if I'll ever get used to all the heels. They pinch my toes and make my heels hurt. No matter, they're fit for a Queen, so getting used to them is a must. I like Sylphina, and though I don't need more than Sigrid because I can dress myself, I kept her on as my lady's maid. Ysella was too cold for my liking. It made me feel uncomfortable. Milori was the one to tell her because I don't like conflict and didn't want to upset her. I recognize this likely doesn't bode well for my authoritative skills as a Queen. Of course, Milori did the task without complaining. He's taken on a big brother role in our relationship, not that I needed another brother hovering around me.

"The Queen Dowager is known for being very kind and wise. Once she meets you, she'll love you like we do!" Sylphina is always so lovely and exuberant, a stark contrast to the rough personality of the Orcs I grew up with or the snakes I used to work for. A rap on the door draws our attention, and the door opens to show my father standing up tall in a brand-new outfit. He's put on some weight in the past week and is finally starting to look like his old self.

"Little Swallow, you look stunning. The old tunic and trousers did you a disservice. This is how you should look." His smile is so genuine and happy. I was afraid he would hate living here, as it's not exactly an Orc village, but he constantly reminds me that wherever Garrick and I are, he'll be 'gladly.'

Sigrid and Sylphina slightly bow to Father, which puts a stupid smile on his face.

"An Orc can get used to all this bowing business." I roll my eyes at him.

"Just what we need, another big-headed Orc wandering around the palace."

"Now, now Emilia, be nice to your brother." Father walks over and wraps his arms around me, squeezing tightly. Pulling away, he glances at himself in the mirror, patting down his silk shirt.

"You look handsome too, Father." He turns to look at me again, pretending to be shocked.

"Of course I do! Have you seen me? The Fae women won't know what to do with all this Orc." A burst of laughter escapes me, as I can hardly catch my breath at his antics. He's never lacked confidence, that's for sure. "Now come, Timas is likely yelling at some poor soul because you're not around to calm him. He's gotten a lot worse this past week. It's silly to wait for this bonding ceremony. Just do it and be done with it. It'll likely make your soon-to-be bonded a lot nicer to deal with."

"I don't know. Milori says he's always this grumpy. Besides, it's only a month away. I'm sure he can handle it. It's not that long." Father snorts at the comment.

"You obviously don't know how agitating it can be, not being with your spirit bond." I don't know how it feels. There's a tendril of annoyance that I feel when Timas isn't around. And I miss him terribly when I haven't seen him for long periods of time, but Father's right. There's no way for me to truly understand how he feels.

"Apparently, the ceremony needs to be meticulously planned because he's the King or something, I don't know." He huffs, taking my arm and placing it in his.

"The Orc tradition is better."

"HA! Right, when Orcs find their Soul Bonds, they throw them over their shoulder and call it good."

"You forget, we go to the temple first. It's not natural to wait so long." I shake my head at him because this is fast for most humans. Even though I was raised by Orcs, I don't feel the same bond they do. It makes it hard to understand. The idea that magic can affect a connection between two people is complex, but either way, I would gladly bond with Timas tonight or a month from now. Father leads us down the hallways, making our way to the ballroom, the same ballroom that was used for the spring festival. We pass some Fae who stare at us. Father smiles, over-exaggerating his large tusks, which scares them so bad they nearly trip over their own feet to get away.

"You know that scares them." He chuckles at the comment.

"I know, but isn't it funny to see them trying to run away? It makes me want to chase after them for fun."

"We're already strange enough. Let's not add to it. A human to be Queen, who was raised by an Orc, who is also wandering around the palace scaring unsuspecting individuals. People talk enough about us."

"Let them talk. We've never cared what others have said about our family." Warmth fills my heart as I remember what he endured to raise Garrick and me. I'll never be embarrassed to be with them. It's a good reminder that no matter what our family looks like, we are, and always will be, family.

"Where's Garrick?" A deep rumble of laughter flows out of him, likely from the residual thought of chasing Fae nobles around the castle.

"He's found himself a distraction in the form of a Fae noblewoman. I can't wait to see what her parents think of an Orc spending time with their daughter. My desire to watch them sputter and slowly die inside is great." Shaking my head at the situation, I can't help but snort. It's one thing for a human to be with a Fae person, but Orc and Fae? No, that's not something that happens. Humans look similar enough to the Fae people, and it's fine in some ways, but the vast majority of Fae can't stand the idea of an Orc being in a relationship with a Fae person. Timas may have to do some damage control later.

We make it to the ballroom entrance, where Timas stands waiting for us. His eyes brighten when he sees me and takes in my outfit. A spark of heat enters his eyes as he walks quickly to me. He gathers me up in his arms as his lips come down on mine. His mouth moves against mine seamlessly and these moments have become increasingly intense between us. Timas says it should settle down after the bonding ceremony (I hope not), but until then, his very being will crave to be with me, some magical way of keeping us together (not that I mind).

"You look ravishing. If only the protocol didn't require us to wait for the full moon to hold the ceremony." He groans as he lays his head on mine.

"We'll make it." I peck his lips quickly and pull away before he gets any ideas.

"I'm standing right here. You couldn't have waited until after I left?" Father mutters as he walks around us and into the ballroom. Timas and I share a smile.

"As much as I would prefer to stay out here and kiss those soft lips again, we should probably head in." I laugh but nod my head. The large oak doors swing open, pushed by the guards on either side, and the room quiets down as we enter. The room looks entirely different from last time. Tonight, there are floating lanterns that give a soft and magical light to the room. Drapes of fine fabric hang from the walls and flow across the ceiling. It's breathtaking.

"Thank you all for coming tonight to celebrate our betrothal! As Fae, we know the value and reverence we have for the spirit bonds. We're not all blessed enough to find one, but the gods saw fit to send me mine, my Emilia. Let tonight be a night of dancing, eating and singing! Let us celebrate together!"

A roar of applause goes up around us as Timas leads me to the centre of the room for a dance. I'm grateful I asked for help on how to dance correctly, or else everyone watching us would know how terrible a dancer I really am. Timas twirls me around the dance floor while the music plays. At the end of the song, as we slow down, I'm nearly out of breath, and we find ourselves searching for a drink. Out of the corner of my eye, I see a woman walking gracefully across the floor as her long, black hair flows behind her. It looks a lot like Timas'. This must be his mother. The knots in my stomach that had been slowly unravelling tighten back up again. She seems to glide over the floor as she walks towards us. Her smile is small, but happiness shines in her eyes. Timas opens his arms and envelopes her.

"Mother, when did you arrive? No one informed me."

"Hello, darling, a couple of hours ago. The boat ride from Casdola was treacherous today." They pull away from each other, and you can see their love for one another.

"You would have been here sooner had you flown." She tuts at him before folding her hands in front of herself.

"You know how it messes up my hair." Timas chuckles, but for some reason, that comment makes her seem more human, and a little of my nerves fade away. Timas steps back and pulls me to his side.

"Mother, this is Emilia. My spirit bond." Her smile widens, and she opens her arms again and hugs me. She feels like happiness. Is that even possible? Her hug is soft, not the tight, bone-crushing one like my father's, and somehow, she exudes motherhood.

"I'm so delighted to meet you finally! Timas hasn't stopped talking about you." My face hurts because of the smile on it. Timas looks back, spotting someone, and gives a nod.

"I need to speak with someone, my flower. Would you mind visiting with my mother for a moment?"

"Of course not." He kisses the top of my head and walks toward Milori and, if I'm not mistaken, a council member, Uldor.

"I don't think I've ever seen him this happy before. Even as a child, he always had a very serious demeanour and kept everyone at arm's length. I don't know how to thank you for making him smile." Timas nods along with whatever conversation they're having.

"He returns the favour daily." She hums in agreement.

"I used to look at my late husband the same way. He brought me so much joy over our time together. It's still hard to believe that he's gone sometimes." Her voice cracks with her words, which pulls my attention to her. I can see the pain written on her face.

"I'm so sorry for your loss." She seems to swallow around the lump in her throat and gives a slight cough before speaking again.

"Thank you, darling. Though we married for political reasons, I fell deeply in love with him. He was my closest friend and confidant. He would curl up on a lounge chair with me and hold me while I read, even though he found the activity immensely boring." Her slight chuckle and faraway gaze suggest that she's reliving a moment from her past.

"I only hope you and Timas can find those quiet moments together. Running this court isn't an easy job. You'll need each other to succeed, and I fear there will be more trouble ahead for both of you."

A feeling of dread washes over me. I'm aware that the court is fighting an unseen adversary, but I'm still struggling to comprehend the significance of Timas' burden. Although they're aware of the culprit behind this, they're still finding it challenging to ensure the safety of the people of Sonas. I can see it taking a toll on Timas daily.

"I don't know if I'll be much help." I stare at Timas, who's been happily talking and laughing with Milori since Uldor left. He deserves someone strong to stand beside him.

"You underestimate your importance. You don't need to be able to fight like the Noble Guard or have a persuasive tongue to change the course of a political meeting. All you need is to be a consistent rock for him. He has enough people in his life telling him what to do, how to do it and who's best suited to do it. What he doesn't have is someone to listen to him because they want to. Someone to love him when he's testy. Someone to support him when everyone else is against him. All he needs is you."

At that moment, Timas throws his head back and laughs at something Milori said. He's worth it. He's worth all of it.

"He was there for me. I'll be there for him."

"I know." She says.

I'm not sure what challenges lie ahead, but I'll stand by Timas and fight for our love and for the Fae people. This land has become my home, and I'll remain loyal to it and to him.

Sneak Peak - Bonded By Intrigue

Emilia

The throne room is a large open space with several pillars lining the sides. The space feels like a garden with vines sprawling up the pillars, around arched windows and embedded into the walls. The marble floor makes the room feel extravagant but I suppose it's supposed to feel that way. The mid-morning sun shines through the stained glass windows creating a dance of colours that float around the room. At the end of the room sit two thrones carved out of dark wood, intricate swirls and several suns cover the chairs. Timas sits on one, his usual royal robes draping over the opulent chair, looking agitated and bored. I can't contain my happiness seeing him. His attention is pulled when he catches sight of me, his blue eyes meet mine and his entire body changes. He sits up straighter and the smile that's reserved for me makes an appearance. Raza'l, one of the council members, is here this morning, likely reporting on the latest murder. The Night Court has ramped up its attacks on Sonas, continuing to cause significant distress in the city, pushing neighbours to suspect each other even though there's no basis for it. Raza'l turns around to see me walking towards them. His already annoyed face morphs into one of disdain. He's been the one on the council most against our pairing; I'm trying not to take that personally.

"My flower!" Timas stands and practically runs to me. His strong arms wrap around me, lifting me straight off the floor. His lips land on mine, making me gasp and moan all at the same time. I push my hands into his hair, feeling the soft, silky strands between my fingers. Wrapped up in his arms, I float away to somewhere else, somewhere where no one is bothered by me being human and the future Queen of the Day Court. Finally, Timas sets me down, breathing heavily, our breaths mingling together.

"I missed you." He whispers.

"You saw me last night," I reply. He groans and tucks his head into my neck.

"Only three more days until you'll be in my arms every night for the rest of our lives." His words are muffled, but they warm me all the same. A cough comes from behind me, and Timas stands straight, his joyful face turning into a mask of defense and indifference.

"Your Majesty, we haven't concluded our business," Raza'l hisses. Timas' eyes begin to darken. Raza'l has become more and more outspoken lately, and Timas' patience is wearing thin. Timas turns slowly, like a snake turning on its enemy. He walks towards Raza'l, and a rumble runs through the room. Raza'l at least has some sense to take a step back.

"You may be part of the council, Raza'l, but you have no right to demand my attention when I'm with my spirit bond. I ask you to remember your place in the future. Just be glad I don't wish to scare my Emilia or I would remind you exactly who you're dealing with."

A brief thought of defiance crosses Raza'l's face, but it doesn't last long. He bows his head apologetically. Before the conversation can continue, the doors to the throne room fling open, and Milori runs into the room.

"Timas! We have guests!" Milori is practically running into the room. The look on his face doesn't shout guests at me. Terror sits behind his eyes. Nearly out of breath, Milori stops in front of Timas.

"What guests?" Timas asks. The anger directed at Raza'l has vanished, and now the stoic King stands before us. Before Milori speaks, he visibly swallows.

"The rightful Queen Neeve of the Night Court. She requests an audience with you. She says she can stop the murders, but she needs your help."

So many thoughts and emotions pass through Timas' eyes. I don't know if he's scared, angry, or confused, but it doesn't take long before he jumps into action.

"Rightful Queen?" Timas asks. Milori just nods his head. "Let's see what she has to say." Timas takes my hand and leads me to the front, sitting me in the chair beside his, the one meant for the Queen. Raza'l nearly bares his teeth at the action, but he catches himself and heads to the side to wait for whatever is about to happen.

The doors are already open when a woman wearing a long, beautiful midnight blue gown and a shining black cloak turns the corner. Holy suns, she's gorgeous. The combination of her pale grey eyes, her long brown hair half-tied back, and her perfect complexion puts me in a trance. Two women follow just behind her in equally lovely gowns, and they practically glide over the floor, whereas I trip over my own feet. She stops several feet from us and looks straight at Timas, not even giving me a side glance. Dipping her head slightly, she returns her gaze to Timas, which is starting to make me feel uncomfortable or murderous, I'm not sure which one.

"Your Majesty."

"I assume you're the one who claims to be the rightful Queen of the Night Court." Timas shifts slightly in his chair, which is the only indication he's ready to fight if he needs to.

"I am." She stands unmoving, like a statue carved from the finest marble, her presence commanding the room with silent dignity.

"Why are you here? As you should be aware, our relationship with the Night Court isn't exactly on good terms. It's rather dangerous of you to walk into the lion's mouth." Timas says. No fear crosses her face, just a look of determination.

"I'm not afraid to be here because I care too much for my people. Right now, my tyrannical half-brother rules the Night

Court, and I intend to get it back. If you can't help me, then I'll find another way, but I'm aware of the issues my half-brother is causing you, and I believe I can solve both of our problems. I hope you'll give me a moment of your time to explain."

Timas looks over at me briefly before returning his attention to Neeve.

"How can you possibly help us when we've been working tirelessly to stop these attacks? What could you possibly offer?"

"I offer this. I can tell you exactly where my half-brother is and how to get there. Navigating the Shrouded Forest isn't an easy feat. I can also share with you how to look out for Night Court spies and the agreement my half-brother has with the Northern Orcs."

"And what do you request in return?"

"I ask that we unite our Courts once more. The exile has done its job. My grandfather is dead, and now, too is my father. My people have lamented over the terrible history of the Night Court uprising. We desire to be united once more and live among each other." Timas pauses before he continues, and a sinking feeling sits in my stomach.

"How do you propose we unite our Courts? And how do I know I can trust you?"

"In terms of trusting me, I can't guarantee anything. It's a chance you'll have to take. As for unification, that's simple. We have a political bonding, uniting our two Courts."

Her words hit me like a slap in the face. The room spins as I grip the arms of the chair. Did she just suggest that Timas bond with her?!

Also by TM Goodkey

The Fae King Series

Fated Mates and Funny Side Characters? Try out this series!

A Spy's Fateful Bond

Bonded By Intrigue

Garrick's Story:

Bonded By Destiny

Milori's Story:

Bonded Across Courts

Acknowledgements

W̲ow, if you are still reading this, then THANK YOU! No, seriously, Thank you! I can't begin to explain how surreal this is. This book would never have happened if my husband hadn't encouraged me to write it and publish it. He also listened to me for hours as I figured out the story, bouncing ideas off him. It really would not have happened without him. Thank you, my love, for believing in me when I stopped believing in myself.

This story also wouldn't have happened without my daughter, Anna, who helped me create the characters.

Thank you to my Alpha readers, Chloe, Wendy and Emma, who read the very rough draft and loved it so much they kept my spark alive, which kept pushing through when my ADHD brain wanted to get distracted.

Thank you, Delanie, for pushing me to figure out social media! Yes, I may be in my thirties, but technology is hard sometimes!

Thank you, Angie, my lovely sister-in-law who helped me edit this thing!

Thank you to my family, who have been huge encouragers of this crazy endeavour!

I feel like I just wrote an Oscar Award thank-you speech! But either way, these people need to be acknowledged because, without them, it wouldn't have happened!

Thank you, READER! You are making this 35-year-old mother of two dreams come true!

If you liked the book, PLEASE give it a review! It really helps me out! Thank you!

About the author

Making dwarves blush, orcs believe in love, and elves lose their cool - that's what TM Goodkey does best. Living in Ontario, Canada, she's beyond happily married with two beautiful children and a backyard full of chickens (which, according to her kids, definitely count as pets). An avid reader of ALL things magical/fantasy with a side of romance, TM has been a published Indie Author since May of 2024. She writes closed door romantasy filled with funny characters, swoony moments, and everything in between.

You can find her here:

Website- www.tmgoodkey.com

Facebook- TM Goodkey Author

Instagram @tmgoodkey